MOTHER
RUSSIA

The Defection of A. J. Lewinter
Sweet Reason
The October Circle

MOTHER
RUSSIA

A Novel by
ROBERT LITTELL

Harcourt Brace Jovanovich
New York and London

Printed in the United States of America

Library of Congress Cataloging in Publication Data

Littell, Robert, 1935-
Mother Russia.

I. Title.
PZ4.L772Mo   [PS3562.I7827]   813'.5'4   77-17014

B C D E

For my first readers,
Ben and Norma Barzman
and Jacques Loyseau

"I've seen the future and it works."
Lincoln Steffens, journalist

"I've seen the future and it needs work."
Robespierre Pravdin, *Homo Economicus*,
hustler, gatecrasher, graffitist.

"*Waak, waak, help, help.*"
Vladimir Ilyich, one of Mother
Russia's feathered friends.

MOTHER
RUSSIA

CHAPTER I

Robespierre Pravdin,
pale as death . . .

Robespierre Pravdin, pale as death, pushes out with the primitively long, broken, badly set thumb of a Cro-Magnon (was he *Homo Economicus* in some previous incarnation?) the cardboard drawer and salutes the bits of wood lined up like cotton-tipped cartridges in an ammunition box.

Q.

Hyphen.

Tips.

Possibilities flicker before his eyes like frames from an old Eisenstein. (Eyeglasses shatter, the baby carriage hurtles down the steps.) He removes one of the sticks and rolls the thin shaft between his deformed thumb and forefinger. Trembling with excitement, he tilts his head and delicately inserts the tip in his ear, extracts it and peers at the orange-brown wax on the cotton. His bloodless lips move, words form but no sound emerges; he is speechless with admiration. The Q-Tip could revolutionize Russia, he feels it in the marrow of his brittle bones. Handled discreetly, it could do for the Russian proletariat what it did for the American proletariat (what it has done for him): stop them from cleaning their ears with their keys!

And he will be the one who did it! Robespierre Isaye-vich Pravdin, the man who brought the Q-Tip to Mother Russia. Hero of Socialist Labor! The Order of the Red Star!! The Order of the Red Banner!!! The Order of Lenin even!!!! (Pravdin wears all four already but he didn't earn them, he found them in the melting snow.) He can almost feel Leonid Ilyich gripping his thin shoulders and pecking like a pigeon at the reddish stubble on each cheek.

It's as plain as the comfortingly long lifeline on his enormous palm: the Q-Tip is an idea whose time has come. Before you can build communism you must construct socialism. Before socialism, an advanced industrial society. And who (the dialogue with himself is becoming animated; he waves the tiny cotton-tipped baton about in the air) ever heard of an advanced industrial society without Q-Tips!

The exquisite logic of it, the scientific *inevitability* of it, makes Pravdin shudder.

Thesis: hard wood.

Antithesis: soft cotton.

Synthesis: (he shouts it out in a voice raw with lust) "The Q-Tip!"

With her resources Russia could close the Q-Tip gap in a matter of months. If the planet is seven-tenths water, Russia is seven-tenths trees. And in the south, Uzbeki gold; Pravdin saw it with his own eyes when he flew down to

Samarkand to pick up some bolts of silk for the wife of the Mexican ambassador and the fermented mare's milk for the Druse: field upon field piled high with mounds (mounds nothing, *mountains!*) of cotton.

So what happens to a hustler with an ingenious idea whose time has come? So what happens is he runs smack into the menopausal monstrosity known as the bureaucracy, that's what happens. Picture it: having dry-cleaned his old Eisenhower jacket for the occasion, Pravdin presents himself at the Ministry of Forestry and pulls from his worn leather briefcase his five-year Q-Tip plan: production statistics (predicated on an increase in consumption of 6 percent a week for the first fifty-two weeks), capital outlay requirements (modest: the wood is there, the cotton is there, it only remains to bring them together), and so forth and so on. Sipping mineral water through glass straws (Pravdin's palm slaps against his high forehead: *Glass straws! Why didn't I think of that?*), the Forestry people play with some figures on a Japanese pocket calculator, double-check the results on a pocket abacus, ask Pravdin if he would mind stepping outside while they kick around the idea. In the end they decide that the Q-Tipsky (as they take to calling it) is essentially a *cotton product.* (So that the day isn't a total loss Pravdin sells them two guaranteed seventeen-jewel Swiss watches, with expanding tarnish-proof chrome wristbands, that register seconds, minutes, hours, months and elapsed time under water.)

A week later Pravdin (casually dropping the Druse's name: *I'm a friend of Chuvash*) organizes an interview with the All-Party Cotton Combine people at the Ministry of Agriculture.

"And what is this O-shaped letter with the little line through the bottom?" inquires a bureaucrat with eyes like tarnished mirrors.

"The capitalists call that a *Q*," Pravdin replies, pronouncing it as if he were trying to cough up a hair at the back of his throat.

"This *Q*," another bureaucrat comes back to it a few minutes later, "what does it represent?" He absently explores his ear with a used Q-Tip. (Pravdin never discards.)

Pravdin's bruised eyes (an impressionistic, not a literal, description; he has seen more than most) flicker uncertainly for an instant. "Because," he explains, appropriately deferential, "in American, cotton begins with *Q*."

Nodding noncommittally, sipping lemonade, the cotton people ask Pravdin if he objects to stepping outside while they analyze the proposal. After a while they summon him back to tell him that the cotton toothpick (as they take to calling it) is at heart a *wood product*.

It's the classic comic all over again! From God knows what obscure reach of his jackpot mentality Pravdin had summoned up this brilliant idea (Hero of Socialist Labor! The Order of the Red Star!! And so forth and so on) to lure youngsters to the Russian classics. *The Brothers Karamazov. Eugene Onegin. War and Peace. Doctor Zhivago* even. (On second thought scratch *Zhivago*.) He turned up at the Artists' Union with an eight-page, four-color pilot of Frolov's Civil War epic, *The Deep Don*. Over glasses of Polish vodka, the bureaucrats pulled on Lenin-like beards and whispered among themselves and decided that the classic comic clearly came under the jurisdiction of the Writers' Union. Over three-star Bulgarian cognac (Pravdin claims to discern a hierarchy based on what bureaucrats *drink*), the Writers' Union people hemmed and hawed and blew their Roman noses into colorful Italian handkerchiefs and decided that the classic comic would more properly come under the authority of the Artists.

Contrary to published reports (see Harold Truman; Pravdin is steeped in history!), the buck never stops.

But Graffiti Pravdin (as he was known before he was expelled from Lomonosov University for antisocialist onanism) is nothing if not tenacious. (Once, in a prison camp near Moscow, he came up with an idea for making shoes from confiscated leather wristwatch straps. They said it couldn't be done but Pravdin collected straps for two and a half years to produce a prototype.) He has a sharpness of mind that pares away extraneous facts; the more he thinks about something the purer it becomes; the purer it becomes the more persistent his pursuit. Acquaintances mistake this persistence for an obsession, especially if they should discover that the project that Pravdin is working on at any given moment has wormed its way, as it often does, into his dreams. The Q-Tips have reached this stage now. For several nights in a row he has had a recurring dream: wearing a chain-mail Eisenhower jacket with medals rattling noisily on the breast, astride an animal he is afraid to identify, he levels his long cotton-tipped lance and charges walls, windmills and in one sequence that left him sweaty and weak and wide awake, Lenin's Tomb! *Well, at least I'm a dreamer,* Pravdin consoles himself as he remembers the numb feeling in the pit of his stomach when he found himself sighting on that holy of holies; *most people are just sleepers.*

Yawning (the result of a late night in the hard currency bar of the Hotel Moskva with two English computer technicians), Pravdin looks at his watches (Japanese, self-winding, they register seconds, minutes, hours, months, fiscal years and diurnal tides in the Philippine Sea) that he wears on top of his cuff because the expanding bands snag the hairs on his wrist. The one set to Moscow time, which has water vapor under the crystal, registers half past. (The other, which has no crystal at all, is set to Greenwich Mean Time; Pravdin feels the need for a standard in his life.) He ransacks the room for his appointment calendar, finds it under a pile of old *Reader's Digests*, confirms the luncheon for the East German editors at the Slaviansky Bazaar. (Pravdin never misses an affair at the Slaviansky if he can help it; they serve Polish, not Russian, vodka, and Georgian sausages that are better than sex.) He pulls on his Eisenhower jacket and basketball sneakers, stuffs his briefcase with Swiss watches, Deutsche Grammophon LP's, American flame-thrower cigarette lighters, Bolshoi tickets, lubricated Swedish condoms, double locks the door of his flat and starts down the wide staircase. The wooden steps creak agreeably under his feet. *Count your blessings*, Pravdin tells himself in what has become a morning ritual. *You're reasonably healthy, relatively wealthy and you live in the next to last wooden house in central Moscow. Touch wood.* (His bony knuckles rap on the polished banister.)

Outside a crowd has gathered around a notice tacked to a tree. (A tree! Lately Pravdin has taken to looking at trees in terms of their component parts: Q-Tips.)

"Come quickly, Robespierre Isayevich," an old woman cries tearfully, "it is the end of the world."

("At the end of the world, go to Bukhara," the Druse once seriously advised him. "Everything happens fifty years later there.")

"How is it they can do this thing?" an elderly man moans. "It is not correct."

The old woman clutches Pravdin's lapels in her bony fingers. "Where will I go?" she croaks. "I've been twenty-seven years here. I shook hands once with Stalin. Tell me, Robespierre Isayevich, what will become of me?"

"What's all the commotion?" demands a bulky lady on her way to the store with a sack of empties.

Pravdin pushes through the crowd to read the notice. His face darkens. "Why, the sons of bitches are tearing down our house," he groans. Everyone turns to stare at the ramshackle wooden structure sandwiched between two concrete apartment buildings.

"To construct what?" the bulky lady inquires.

"What else, to construct Socialism," Pravdin fires back. He pulls a Western felt-tipped pen from his breast pocket and scrawls across the notice:

Quis custodiet ipsos custodes?

Setting her mouth into a tight line, the bulky lady adjusts her reading glasses. "Defacing a public notice is against the law," she scolds. Chin elevated, eyes peering through thick lenses, she reads Pravdin's footnote. "What language is this, Jewish?"

"Jewish is right, lady," Pravdin stage whispers. "It's an old Talmudic saying that means, 'Who will watch the bosses?' "

"Attention," snaps the bulky lady. The empties in her sack jingle as she gestures. "Those who are not with us are considered to be against us."

Pravdin winks slyly. "Under capitalism, man exploits man. Yes or no?"

The bulky lady nods warily. "Yes."

"Under communism," Pravdin assures her, "it is just the opposite!"

The bulky lady moves away uncertainly, hesitates, returns like a tide and tries to drown Pravdin in accusations. Her voice, shrill as a cat's in heat, echoes through the alleyway. Necks crane. Heads wrapped in dust kerchiefs dart from windows. Pravdin, who was born with his inner ear tuned to proscenium wavelengths, practically dances as he denies that he is a radish-Communist (red outside, white inside). "The bosses don't see eye to eye with me," he concedes, "but do I hold it against them?" ("Neither for, neither against, as God is my witness," he assured the Druse the first time they met. The Druse always has to know where a man stands politically before he will do business with him.)

The bulky woman raps her knuckles on the notice, gestures toward the house, jabs her index finger into Pravdin's solar plexus. "It's ones like you . . ."

Pravdin retreats. "Talking politics is like talking about life after death," he murmurs. "I have thank you enough trouble with life before death."

The crowd breaks up (reluctantly; Muscovites don't particularly want to get where they are going). Folding himself into his dignity as if it is an old Army greatcoat, Pravdin hurries off toward the Slaviansky. On the path that runs parallel to the Moscow River he pauses alongside the Kremlin wall to light a cigarette, then quickly scribbles with a piece of chalk:

I've seen the future and it needs work

(L. Steffens: Pravdin never forgets a face or a phrase). His spirits buoyed, he cuts through the Kremlin with a group of German tourists, tries (unsuccessfully) to sell Bolshoi tickets to the stragglers, stops under the clock in the Kremlin tower (which is two minutes slow) to buy a lottery ticket but doesn't find a number that suits him. Ten minutes later he is at the entrance to the Slaviansky Bazaar, a restaurant remarkable (in addition to its Polish vodka and Georgian sausages) for its prerevolutionary decor.

"Pravdin, Robespierre Isayevich," he announces to the lady wrestler with the guest list, "at your beck and call."

She takes in his basketball sneakers, his trousers frayed at the cuffs from walking on them, his Eisenhower jacket with the four medals overlapping above the breast pocket, his day-old growth of rust-colored beard, she runs her polished thumbnail down the *P*'s. "There is no Pravdin," she says cautiously.

"But there is, ravishing lady; you have the honor of having him before your very original body." Pravdin gives her a fleeting glimpse of a small laminated card (the menu from a Leningrad ice-cream parlor), mumbles something about representing the Second Chief Directorate of GLUBFLOT.

"Oh dear," the woman says nervously. Pravdin smiles crookedly (according her a glimpse of stainless steel bicuspids), bows, brushes past her into the Slaviansky.

The first person he runs into is another freeloader, his old camp friend Friedemann T., a goateed painter who claims to have created abstract socialist realism. He is wearing a dark tapered suit (French), pointed shoes (Greek), a white-on-white shirt (Russian) with studs (his grandfather's) and a light prewar overcoat (origin obscure) draped over delicately hunched shoulders.

"What are we here?" the painter whispers urgently, a glass of vodka in one hand, a Georgian sausage in the other. "Computers?"

"What we are is literary," Pravdin whispers back, plucking a glass of vodka from a passing tray.

"Literary." Friedemann T. takes this in. He lifts on his toes, sways as if he is putting himself into gear, raises the pitch of his voice. "What's wonderful in a book, if you want my view, is what the author doesn't say." He bites into the sausage and washes it down with a mouthful of vodka.

"In my new novel," Pravdin offers—neither bothers looking at the other—"I'm experimenting with action that has no relation at all to character."

"Not possible," Friedemann T. dismisses the idea out of hand. "Action *is* character."

"The trouble with that," complains Pravdin, "is there's no way for a character to step out of character. Whatever he does, he is. My God, that's worse than solitary confinement!" Through ventriloquist's lips he adds:

"Where are they hiding the sausages?"

The painter motions with his head and they casually move off in that direction. "Mind you, his work is splendid," the painter loudly confides. He nods at a famous editor, who looks back blankly. "If it has a fault it is that he doesn't empty himself. When I work I always go to great pains to empty myself." Friedemann T. snorts. "Quietly, it goes without saying, so as not to make waste or noise."

"In thirty-four I think it was," Pravdin reaches back into his memory, "Isaac Emanuilovich told the First Congress of Soviet Writers, 'I have invented a new genre—the genre of silence.' "

Friedemann T. belches; his overcoat falls to the floor. Pravdin restores it to his shoulders. "The genre of silence!" the painter remarks. "I'll bet you wish you'd said that."

"I will," Pravdin promises.

On their way out Friedemann T. consults his pocket calendar, reminds Pravdin about a midafternoon vernissage at the Artists' Union and a dinner symposium of geologists at the Rossiya. "The geologists are serving chicken Kiev," he reminds him, "and a decent Bulgarian wine."

"It is not possible," Pravdin tells him regretfully. "Apartment hunting is what I am obliged to do." He explains about the notice tacked to the tree.

"They're not going to tear down that beautiful building of yours?" Friedemann T. whistles. "Aesthetically speaking, that could qualify as a crime. There aren't five like it left in central Moscow."

"After this one goes there won't be but one; mine is the next to last," Pravdin says wistfully. "A vacant apartment by any chance you don't know of? My requirements are modest: sunlight, space, calm, privacy and discreet neighbors."

Friedemann T. shakes his head gloomily. "If I knew of such a place I would move in myself. Why don't you approach the Druse?"

"No, no, for small things I don't like to bother him," Pravdin insists.

"Since when is an apartment a small thing?"

"For the Druse," Pravdin assures him, "it is."

Pravdin, twenty minutes early, is hoping to be the first on line; he is forty-first. He comforts himself by thinking of those ahead as potential clients.

"How do I know these tickets are genuine?" demands a middle-aged woman wrapped in an enormous brown shawl.

"How does she know these tickets are genuine?" Pravdin repeats innocently. "Yes or no? Under socialism, forgery is a state crime but hustling is a state necessity?"

The woman laughs self-consciously. "I'll take two," she says and carefully counts out eight rubles from her wallet. Pravdin folds the money away in his change purse.

Behind Pravdin two young men are playing chess on a pocket board. White advances his queen's bishop to knight five. "If I say Schönberg," he complains, "you say Webern; if I say chromatic equality is a built-in tenet of serialism, you opt for diatonic species."

"I couldn't help overhearing," Pravdin intrudes. "What a coincidence you speak of Schönberg. I happen to have on my very person some Deutsche Grammophon discs that arrived only last night from West Germany."

When Pravdin's turn comes he finds himself face to face with the most expressionless human he has ever set eyes on in his life.

"Next," the woman says, glancing up from her incredibly organized desk at a wall electric clock that has no hour hand. Like Pravdin she is extremely thin; unlike Pravdin she is thin without being frail. "Next," she repeats tonelessly, impatiently, tapping a front tooth with a fingernail.

Pravdin hands her the form he has filled out, along with his Moscow residence permit (it cost a small fortune), his internal passport, a letter (forged) certifying he is a member in good standing of the Writers' Union and therefore is entitled to twice the standard nine square meters of living space that is the inalienable right of every Soviet citizen, and a military certificate (the genuine article) indicating he suffers from an old war wound and therefore is entitled to live within a radius of a hundred meters of public transportation. Methodical in her movements the woman piles up the documents, begins with the internal passport, glances at the word *Jew* penned in alongside entry three (ethnic origin), pockets the two Bolshoi tickets Pravdin has discreetly placed in the military certificate.

The interview, Pravdin senses, is off to a reasonable start. Touch wood.

"What is the nature of your war wound?" the thin woman asks in a voice that conveys total lack of interest in the answer.

"Shrapnel in the neck," Pravdin explains. "Pinched nerves. I lost the ability to shrug."

"That doesn't sound incapacitating," comments the thin woman.

"Incapacitating is what it is," Pravdin argues passionately. "In a workers' paradise the inability to shrug is the ultimate wound." Pravdin leans across the desk. "Lovely lady," he pleads, "I have friends in high places. I could use influence, but I don't take advantage of my name, I wait my turn like any ordinary citizen."

The thin woman shuffles through some file cards. "I can offer you a flat in Dzerzhinsky—"

"Sooner Siberia!" blurts Pravdin.

"Dzerzhinsky is twenty-five minutes by metro from the Kremlin," the woman continues tonelessly. "The flat is in a building with an elevator, it is eighty-five meters from a metro station, it has fourteen square meters surface, heat, hot water and kitchen privileges—"

"I'm entitled to eighteen square meters," Pravdin whines.

The woman shrugs, writes the address on a card, stamps the card with a seal and signs her name across the seal, hands it to Pravdin, looking up at him for the first time.

"Could I trouble you," Pravdin says with mock formality, "for the return of my Bolshoi tickets."

"What tickets," the thin woman asks innocently, "are you talking about?"

Pravdin paces off the distance from the metro to the front door of the gray building, six stories, one of many in a suburban project set at angles that suggest they are giving each other the cold shoulder. People stare. Pravdin concentrates, loses count, starts again, is annoyed to find the total eighty-three.

The occupants of the flat, a worn, tired man with thinning hair and his pregnant wife, are wrapping dishes in newspaper and packing them in cartons when Pravdin knocks. (A note indicates the bell is out of order.)

"You're the new tenant then," the man assumes. He manages a smile. "Come on, I'll give you the royal tour."

"First the lowdown on the building," Pravdin demands. His eyes, darting nervously, take in the room: boxes tied and ready to go, matching overstuffed easy chairs, a grandfather clock with a sweep second hand that jerks when it passes the five, a huge television set, trunks, suitcases.

The pregnant woman straightens, her palms on the small of her back. "I have to admit it, the building has a certain charm," she observes dryly. "Today for instance there was no cold water in the taps. You wouldn't be interested in a kitchen table, would you? The top is genuine formica."

Pravdin, dispirited, shakes his head, shuffles around the room, peeks into the kitchen, the toilet (both shared with another family), sniffs, screws up his face in disgust, tries to flush the toilet, has to climb on the handle to depress it. Using the tip of his sneaker he pushes up the yellowing plastic toilet seat; it is angled badly and bangs down again.

"How do you pee?" Pravdin asks absently.

"Quickly," the man replies.

"Funny is what you're not," snaps Pravdin. He turns on the tap marked "cold"; rusty hot water gushes out. He looks up at the shower nozzle, which is caked with a whitish residue, and then down at the hole in the cement floor that serves as a drain.

"I suppose the facilities are like this in our space rockets," the pregnant woman clucks her tongue sympathetically. Her husband shoots her a look and she goes back to her packing.

"The same is what it is," Pravdin agrees, "with the possible exception that the drain holes are stainless steel."

"Listen, it's not all that bad," the tired man urges. "The couple you share the kitchen with, the woman works at the hard currency store for tourists and gets the inside track on certain shipments before they're put on sale."

"She's good on fur hats, leather gloves, waterproof boots," the wife calls out.

But Pravdin is already removing his sinking heart from the flat.

There are no signs forbidding people to walk on the grass; none are needed. But Pravdin, hunched forward, absorbed in his thoughts as he cuts diagonally across Sokolniki Park, is in no mood to obey signs that aren't there. Pigeons scatter. Emaciated squirrels claw their way up trees. An old man in civilian clothes with a chest full of medals angrily shakes his cane but Pravdin, out of earshot, hurtles on. At Khokhlovka, a district of factories and warehouses, he reaches for his chalk, scrawls in English across a billboard trumpeting how many schools have been built in the last five years:

Nothing worth knowing can be teached

(Anon: Pravdin studied English in the camps but his teacher disappeared in midcourse). Glancing fearfully at dark clouds conspiring over the rooftops, he hurries on to the warehouse that serves the Druse as a base of operations.

The small door at the rear opens before he has a chance to ring. Pravdin, shivering from a rain that has yet to fall, ducks to enter, is greeted by Zosima, a Berber with a small blue flower tattooed on her left cheek. Long plaits of silky black hair fall across her shoulders to her waist, indicating that she is not married. Her lids are painted blue; her gaze is direct, unblinking. Pravdin has seen her before; she is one of the Druse's "nieces" and chauffeurs him around in a curtained Packard that is said to have belonged to the Cuban ambassador. ("I never drive myself," the Druse once confided to Pravdin, "my hands are too small.")

"Chuvash expects you," murmurs Zosima.

"How expects me?" Pravdin is edgy. "I never called I was coming."

Zosima only steps back, bolts the door behind him,

leads the way through labyrinthian warehouse aisles stacked with busts and statues of men whose biographies have been conveniently lost: Bukharin, Trotsky, Kamenev, Zinoviev. ("I am the day watchman at a pantheon of nonpersons," the Druse told Pravdin the first time he visited the warehouse.)

The Druse, whose full name is Chuvash Al-hakim bi'amrillahi, greets Pravdin at the door of the room that serves the warehouse guardian as an office. Dressed in a black European suit, an embroidered skullcap set squarely on his shiny bald scalp, deeply tanned, he places his right hand on his heart, inclines his head to Pravdin. "*Salaam aleikum,* brother," he says quietly.

"*Shalom Aleichem* back to you." Pravdin bows awkwardly, precedes the Druse into his office which is covered, floors and walls, in oriental carpets, giving to the room the thick muffled atmosphere of an Uzbek *yourta*. Chuvash and Pravdin sit cross-legged on either side of a low iron table. An old beetlelike woman, her face masked by a heavy black horsehair veil, hovers. Chuvash mutters something to her in Kirghiz (one of the six Turkic dialects he speaks fluently). She moves away, neither man speaks, she returns with shallow bowls of green tea brewed in a charcoal-heated samovar and served with a delicate herb called *hell*. The aroma clears Pravdin's nasal passages. The Druse offers Pravdin a plate of biscuits. He takes one, bites into it, cups his other hand underneath to catch the crumbs.

The Druse sips his tea while it is still scalding hot. Pravdin leaves his bowl on the table and blows on it until he can bear to lift it. When the bowls are empty the old woman is summoned to take them away.

"So." Pravdin dries his lips on the sleeve of his Eisenhower jacket, clears his throat.

"Brother, it has come to me again," Chuvash says.

Pravdin, concealing his skepticism behind a crooked smile, leans forward.

Chuvash places both hands on the iron table, palms down, speaks with his eyes closed, his back straight. "It is the reign of the last Emir of Bukhara, Said Mirmuhammed Alimkhan," he recounts intently. "He lives in the Ark twenty meters above the level of the city. This Friday, as every Friday, carpets are laid between the Ark and the mosque. The people prostrate themselves, see only the Emir's finely worked golden slippers as he makes his way to the mosque. Later he returns to the Ark through the twin towers, mounts the tunnel between the prison cells, pauses to say something to a dignitary just before my door. I see him through a crack in the wood. He is a slight man, absolutely beardless. When he speaks to the dignitary I become aware that he has a stutter. 'That the executions b-b-b-b-begin,' he commands. The dignitary falls to his knees to kiss the hem of his robe. The Emir continues on to the balcony to watch the executions. This Friday there are five. They are performed with a knife. I am to be the fourth."

"How can you be sure it's you?" Pravdin, agitated, demands.

"In the vision I am brought to the courtyard below the balcony. They are dragging away the corpse of the man before me; he had been convicted of incest. I fall on my knees and lift my palms to the Emir for mercy. And I see on my palm the triangle of lines indicating I am a seer." Chuvash turns up his right palm and traces the triangle with his finger. "You see, it is always the same."

"What about the mercy?" Pravdin wants to know.

"The Emir smiles down at me and nods in a kindly, almost fatherly, way just as the executioner's knife slices through my jugular."

"Aiiiiiiii," Pravdin grimaces, clutching his own throat; he has a vivid imagination and a low threshold of pain.

Chuvash smiles. "It is fascinating, is it not? If there were only a way to study this phenomenon scientifically, to confirm it—"

"How many of these incarnations have you had?" asks Pravdin.

"It is difficult for me to say. Often different visions seem to relate to the same incarnation. I count at least six, but I'm not certain. And you?" Chuvash gestures with his pinky nail, which he has allowed to grow extremely long. "I understand you don't consider them evidence of previous incarnations as I do, but have you had any more of your dreams?"

Pravdin flashes his crooked smile. "I dreamed about a monastery cell, whitewashed. The bunk bed has no pillow, the crucifix above it has been pried off but it has left its imprint from having been there for centuries. A bearded Jew of indeterminate age leans against the imprint of the crucifix."

"Ah," sighs Chuvash, impressed.

"It is only a dream," cautions Pravdin.

"Of course," Chuvash nods. "Continue."

"Shots ring out, a ragged volley first, then a single shot from a smooth-bored naval pistol. The Jew starts, opens his eyes, sees for the first time the imprint of the crucifix. His bloodless lips move, words form but no sound emerges; he is speechless with humiliation. A horrified expression crawls across his face like a crab. At that instant a key turns in the lock, the door swings open with a squeal."

"Who is it?"

"Who it is I will never know," Pravdin confesses. "Someone flushed the communal toilet, the pipes banged and I woke up."

Zosima slips into the room, whispers to the Druse. He

produces a huge gold pocket watch, sees it has stopped, taps it with his pinky nail to make it start, says a few words in Uighur. Zosima backs out of the room.

The Druse appears pressed for time. "What brings you to me, brother?" he asks politely.

Pravdin laughs nervously. "What brings me to you is a favor."

"Only ask it," Chuvash instructs him.

Pravdin hesitates long enough to suggest he doesn't relish asking favors, then tells him about the tearing down of the next to last wooden house in central Moscow.

Chuvash pulls a scrap of paper from a pocket, uncaps a pen, jots a name and phone number on the paper, offers it to Pravdin. "If they are forcing you out of the next to last wooden house in central Moscow, there is only one place for you: the *last* wooden house in central Moscow. Call this number, ask for a man by this name, speak to no one else, say only that you are a friend of Chuvash Al-hakim bi'am-rillahi."

Stunned at the ease of it all Pravdin accepts the paper, folds it away between the bills in his change purse. "When I can do something for you only ask," he promises the Druse.

"When you can do something for me," Chuvash replies evenly, "you will know it without my asking."

CHAPTER 2

The last wooden house
in central Moscow . . .

The last wooden house in central Moscow, two floors of
frayed eaves and awnings, looms at the dead end of an
L-shaped alley off Trubnaya Square. Pravdin, nostalgic for
the ordered sweetness of shtetl life he has never experienced,
blinks back a rush of emotion as he sets down his rope-
bound cardboard suitcases. Dear God in heaven, a building with soft edges and no right angles! Surrounded by a
fence! White birch trees! Shrubbery! A garden! Weeds even!
Next door, the faded paint peeling from its onion-shaped
domes: a sixteenth-century Orthodox church that has been
converted into a wine shop. Across the alley, towering over
both the church and the wooden house: a line of prewar

apartment houses, their backs to the alley, their windows silvery with reflected sunlight. Pravdin, fighting faintness, rests a hand on a birch to steady himself. Birds chirp. The sound of Mozart hangs in the air like moisture. The alley seems to swallow Pravdin as he approaches the house, swings back the wooden gate. Hinges squeal. *Count your blessings,* Pravdin almost weeps. *You're reasonably healthy, relatively wealthy and you're moving into the last wooden house in central Moscow. Touch wood.* (His knuckles rap against the wooden fence.)

"Hello to anyone?" Pravdin hollers into the house, holding open the front door. "Someone home?"

"Hello yourself," a female voice calls from one of the ground-floor rooms. A moment later a young girl pads into the hall on bare feet. She has long matted blonde hair that falls to her waist, wears an American sweat shirt with "Make Amends" embroidered across the breast and jeans that flare at the ankle. She appears to be about fifteen. "I'm Ophelia Long Legs," she supplies, cocking her head, studying Pravdin with childlike curiosity. "You must be the new attic. Wow! What a fantastic jacket. Where'd you ever find it?"

"It's an old Eisenhower jacket," Pravdin starts to explain.

"What's Eisenhower? Say, do you eat meat?"

"What kind of a question is that, 'Do you eat meat?' "

"I don't mean to be nosey." Ophelia Long Legs glances up the stairs, lowers her voice. "The reason why I ask is because the ladies you share the kitchen with are vegetarians and they can't support the smell of meat." Ophelia giggles. "We don't eat meat either but that's because we can't afford it."

"Who's 'we'?" Pravdin, always on the alert for new clients, wants to know.

" 'We' is whoever happens to be in the room. We're *volosatiye*—hairy ones—you see. Friends come, friends go. Some stay a day, some stay a month."

"What about residence permits? What about the police?"

"Oh, the militia gives us a wide berth," Ophelia boasts. She whispers again. "Some of us have fathers who are *vlasti*—you know, bosses. What's your name anyhow?"

"Pravdin, Robespierre Isayevich," Pravdin draws himself up, soundlessly clicking the heels of his sneakers together, "at your beck and call."

"Hey, that's cute," Ophelia giggles, looking at the sneakers. "What kind of a nutty name is Robespierre? It doesn't sound Russian."

"It's French. A famous French revolutionary is whom I was named after," Pravdin explains.

"I thought France was capitalist," the girl says innocently. "Say, you wouldn't happen to have any French rock records, would you?"

"I know where I can put my hands on some," Pravdin ventures cautiously, "but they're for sale, not for lend."

"Oh, we've got money when it comes to records, don't you worry your head about that."

Pravdin drags his suitcases into the hall as the girl holds open the door. "What's the lowdown on the building?" he demands.

"There are a couple of drips on this floor," Ophelia replies. "The man who lives there is an embalmer." Her face screws up in disgust. "They say he's the one who bathes *Diadya* Lenin every other week. A genuine general has that room. A limousine with the tiniest flag on the fender you ever saw comes to get him every morning. That must mean he's important, mustn't it? And the weatherman lives there with his girl friend who's not here now because she's having marital problems with her husband. The weatherman is neat; he's the one on television every night with the weather report, the one with the cute mustache. Upstairs there's Mother Russia and Nadezhda. And you. Mother Russia is a super lady."

Ophelia leans toward Pravdin's ear. "She's a bit off her head actually, but it's nothing serious. She believes in flying saucers and visitors from outer space and things like that. You'll get along with her just fine if you know what she likes and what she doesn't like. She's kind of old and fussy and fixed in her ways, if you know what I mean."

Pravdin, a collector of idiosyncrasies as well as things, settles down on a suitcase. "What does she like and not like, then?"

Ophelia thinks a moment. "She doesn't like germs, telephones, the Singer Sewing Machine Company, knocks on the door, starch in shirts or sheets, General Shuvkin,"— Ophelia indicates the General's door—"meat, sneezing because it lets the soul escape, insane asylums, lightning and electric samovars. As for what she likes: there's fresh snow, getting letters and writing them, all things the color of absinthe, exotic tea, parrots, wood, Akhmatova, softness, craziness and me. She likes me," Ophelia laughs happily. "And what is it you don't like, Comrade Eisenhower?"

Pravdin remembers some words from a poem. "What I don't like is mist, bell sounds and brokenness," he replies.

"Hey, you'll get along fine," Ophelia concludes brightly. "Come on, I'll introduce you to Mother Russia. I'm dying to see how she'll react to someone with a name like Robespierre."

Ophelia grabs one of Pravdin's suitcases and drags it up the wooden stairs ahead of him. "Zoya Aleksandrovna," she calls. "Come look—your new attic is here." Laughing merrily, she tosses back at Pravdin: "Wait until she hears about your mist, bell sounds and brokenness."

Zoya Aleksandrovna Volkova emerges from her room and leans over the banister under a skylight. She is dressed in pleated trousers, sturdy walking shoes with low heels and laces, a man's shirt, wears two ragged silver fox pieces around her neck to guard against chills, carries a fly swatter tucked under her arm. Her hair, twisted into a bun, is gray.

"Charmed," she says in a suspicious voice, leaning over the railing to offer Pravdin her hand, palm down. He reaches up and takes it, is uncertain whether to kiss it or shake it; he is struck by her skin, which is soft with age and doesn't seem to be attached to the bones.

"Greetings to you, little mother," he offers politely.

Mother Russia draws Pravdin's hand to her bifocals, raises her head to study his nails through the lower lens. "Good, good, you don't at all appear to be communistical. Here, child, regard the paleness of his nails; it indicates melancholy for certain, persecution maybe. The broadness"— Mother Russia's thumb polishes each of his nails as she proceeds along his hand—"is a positive sign, yes, it means he's not, thanks God, ambitious. (Only fools are ambitious is what I think. But that's another story.) Ah, the white mark is *mauvais, mauvais*, means misfortune, poor dear." She looks up suddenly into his face. "What is your given name?"

"Robespierre, little mother."

"Robes-pierre." She tries it, then shifts the accent. "Robes-pierre. Yes, I like it better, don't you, that way. Robes-pierre. Well, God grant you don't end up the way he did." She releases his hand, sniffs the air. "You don't I hope to God have any communicable diseases, do you?"

"He looks as white as a sheet," Ophelia comments.

"No, no, perfectly healthy is what I am," Pravdin protests. "Pale is how I always look. Hustlers, like Hasidim, avoid the sun. Take my word for it, little mother, from me there's nothing you can catch."

"*Tant mieux*," she tosses over her shoulder, heading for

the kitchen and indicating with a flick of her fly swatter that he is to follow.

"You're in the attic, up those stairs. The toilet's here. Each of us expected to buy paper whenever we find it, Scandinavian brands preferred. They're more, excuse the expression, absorbent. As for the kitchen, I suppose Ophelia told you about no meat. No meat includes no chicken. No meat. No chicken. Fish, eggs, grains, herb teas of all sorts. Here" —Mother Russia thrusts into Pravdin's hands a eucalyptus branch—"put this on your windowsill, it will discourage the mosquitoes. When you're unpacked call me; whatever you do, don't knock at my door; never knock at my door. I invite you for an infusion. We will have a conversation, you and I; perhaps we will the both of us together figure out why you have come to us."

"I have come to you only to live, little mother," Pravdin says, puzzled.

But Mother Russia only smiles as if she knows better.

Pravdin unpacks his belongings, folds away his khaki shirts on the top shelf of the closet, lays out his toilet articles on the shelf over the small washbasin in his room, disinfects the basin with alcohol that he pours on and ignites. He finds a broom in a kitchen closet and sweeps the attic. From under a dresser he collects a pile of sawdust. *Termites!* he thinks, horrified. He pulls out the drawers one by one and examines the interior. Nothing. He gets down on his knees and examines the under side. On the inside of one of the legs he finds a layer of wood plaster. He tests it with his fingertip. The plaster is dry, but behind it there is a small hollow. Pravdin leans back on his haunches, wipes away with his sleeve the sweat that has accumulated on his forehead. Suddenly he shudders. *Why,* he asks himself, struggling for calm, for logic, for perspective, *why would they put a microphone in my room? What is it they expect to hear?* He is tempted to talk into it, to tell them he knows it's there, to take a knife and pry it out and fling it from the window (open, with the eucalyptus branch on the sill). But an old camp instinct tells him:

A microphone you are aware of is something you can fill with silence.

Pravdin, his pinky angled off into space, sniffs at the infusion, which has been sweetened with small chunks of green apple, as if it is medicinal.

"Drink up," Mother Russia orders. She hovers over him, tapping her leg impatiently with the fly swatter. "Water lily roots are excellent for the circulation. Judging from the paleness of your skin you could use with a little circulation. Exhale first so you won't smell it. That's the way. Now drink. And be careful how you handle my china. Let me see, where was I before I interrupted myself?"

She inserts a cigarette in a long ivory holder, lights up. The holder bobs as she speaks. "Ah, I was in Lvov. I saw only five cats during the five years I lived in Lvov—all at the same time! They were all, God bless them, black. It was just before they came for my husband. I took it as an omen: five black cats crossing your path at once! They belonged if I remember correctly to a fat Germanic housewife; she was plodding toward her back door with an armload of kindling, surrounded by an honor guard of five equally fat cats, tails en chandelle (you do speak French, don't you?), weaving gracefully about her. I dropped what I was doing and hurried home to warn him—too late, too late." Mother Russia sighs; tears well in her eyes. "Don't mind me," she says, angry at herself. "I always cry at holocausts." She blows her nose into a paper napkin. "In Petersburg I met a gray and white tom near the Voznessensky Bridge reeling home after a night in the coal cellars. He hoarsely conversed with me for several minutes, then went on his drunken way. I took that as an omen too and the next day the Germans attacked. Do you like cats, Robes-pierre Isayevich?"

"I like their taste, little mother," Pravdin tells her, exhaling as she directed and trying another sip of infusion.

"Their taste!" Mother Russia gulps her own infusion between short puffs on her long ivory holder. "Did I understand you to comment on their taste?"

"In the camps, little mother, any cat we got our hands on we ate. Thinking of them as pets was a luxury I never had."

"So you're from the camps then." Mother Russia contemplates Pravdin's badly set thumb through a haze of cigarette smoke. "I have put in a certain amount of time too," she says quietly. "But that's another story."

They are silent for a while. Pravdin grows accustomed to the water lily root infusion and drinks from his cup more willingly. When he finishes she invites him to her room off the kitchen.

"*Waak, waak, power to the powerful, power to the powerful.*"

Pravdin ducks, pivots, throws up before his face a protective mesh of fingers, finds himself staring through the mesh into the beady eyes of a green-crested parrot who stirs the air with his wings in greeting.

"Gently, gently, Kerensky," Mother Russia calms the bird, chucking him under the beak with the swatter end of her fly swatter.

Pravdin, recovered, takes in the room: large with an alcove, light pouring in through a birch tree, three golden cages containing three green-crested parrots hanging at different heights from an ornate ceiling, a large overhead electric fan that doesn't work, a brass four-poster (unmade, with the imprint of a small body on one side, as if leaving a place for someone to sleep next to her), a night table covered with books and bottles of herbs and powders, an old prewar Singer sewing machine, worn carpets underfoot, an old gramophone, a 1930s art deco table clock ticking away perfectly, a collection of 78 r.p.m. records, a desk with an old Cyrillic Remington on it, piles of papers, books everywhere, dozens of postcards (yellow and curling at the edges) thumbtacked to the wall above the desk.

"I collected them as a child," Mother Russia explains, "when it was an everyday occurrence to receive such things from outside the country in the mail. My father, a fur salesman during one period of his life, traveled a great deal and sent me a card from every city he visited. See"—the fly swatter becomes a pointer—"Istanbul was called Constantinople then; Izmir, Smyrna. You are to sit here." She plants herself across from Pravdin at a small round table covered with a rectangular cloth with fringes that reach to the floor. "Serve yourself," she nods toward a bowl of grapes.

Pravdin selects a small bunch, clips it from the stem with a silver scissors, dips the grapes into a cut-glass bowl, half full of water and a slice of lemon, spits the pits into his palm and deposits them in a heavy cut glass ashtray.

"Waak, waak, rev-lutions are verbose."

"Another bird heard from," Mother Russia comments. "That one's named Trotsky. The third one is Vladimir Ilyich Lenin. I suspect Vladimir Ilyich of homosexual tendencies—the bird, not the man. I have seen him at various times eyeing both Kerensky and Trotsky with that watery stare often associated with sex."

Pravdin fidgets uncomfortably. "What does Vladimir Ilyich say?"

"Oh, he's the least talkative of the three," Mother Russia allows. She reaches through the cage with her swatter and taps Vladimir Ilyich on the head.

"*Help, help, waak, waak.*"

Pravdin flashes one of his crooked smiles. "Funny birds are what they are," he comments.

"The originals were funny birds too," Mother Russia says. "I knew them, you know. I knew them all. Ha! I am an old anti-Bolshevik. Kerensky was a fiery speaker but a prude. His fingernails were a walking disaster: narrow, indicating ambition; ingrown too, a sign of luxurious tastes. Oh, I had a certain respect for him in the beginning, I will admit it to you. He was caught between two immense forces neither of which he really understood, neither of which he could have controlled even if he had understood them. For a long time I saw him as that modern existential hero, the man in the middle. But all that ended when he scurried from a back door of the Winter Palace, skirts whipping around his thick ankles, as the Bolsheviks stormed through the front door. Enter Trotsky! He was always nasty and needling. His nails were as pale as yours, come to think of it, though they were much smaller than yours; small nails mean conceit. Vladimir Ilyich was by far the least sexy of the three. His nails were broad, indicating a timidness that was only apparent to those who had the misfortune to be close to him, and round, indicating a generous liberal spirit underneath the hard pragmatic exterior. When I was a child Lenin hid in my father's apartment in Petersburg. I remember it as if it were yesterday. (I consider memory a form of time travel. But that's another story.) Lenin, looking ridiculously like a female impersonator in his red wig, presented himself at our door. Mother had no idea who he was and obliged him to walk on canvas rectangles to polish the floors. She made us all walk on the canvas, even father. When I was sixteen I entered the living room one day walking directly on the floor. I remember the clickety-click of my Paris heels on the tiles. Conversation stopped. It was my great moment of revolt, more important even than when I parted with my virginity, which I organized the following year. My mother looked down at my shoes and then at my father, but my father continued reading his newspaper. I never walked on canvas again."

"And Lenin?" Pravdin demands curiously.

"Lenin," Mother Russia rummages for memories, "seemed to me like an old woman, shuffling around like that in a wrinkled robe polishing my mother's floors. He stayed three days and spent a great deal of time in the bathroom; his intestines were not in any condition to make a revolution. People came and went. My mother ran out of canvas and made them walk about in their stockings. Her floors shone like they had never shone before. Trotsky was embarrassed to remove his shoes and had to be asked several times. He had holes in his stockings, you see. There was whispering late into the night. One man raised his voice and banged a table with his fist and everyone shushed him. Lenin shuffled back and forth on the canvas and said, 'All right, what do we have to lose,' and went off to the toilet. Through the worst of the Civil War someone appeared at our flat twice a week with a basket of bread, some eggs, a bottle of jam, tea and an endless supply of pamphlets."

"Waak, rev-lutions are verbose, waak, waak."

Pravdin's lust for the theater gets the upper hand. Thrusting an imaginary microphone across the table in a parody of an eager TV reporter, he blurts: "In your opinion, Zoya Aleksandrovna, what is the difference between our life today and the days before the Revolution?"

Mother Russia responds instantly to the game. "Ha!"

she cackles, "the greatest difference is there are fewer birds in the trees today. And fewer trees. But that's another story."

"Waak, waak, *help, help,*" barks Pravdin.

By the time Nadezhda arrives home, just before dinner, they are on their fifth glass of rose hip wine (Mother Russia's own concoction) and carrying on like long lost friends.

"Picture it," Pravdin cries, folding himself into a comic crouch. "After four hours on line the guard asks me, 'What are you waiting for, comrade?' So what do I tell him? So what I tell him is: 'For the state to wither away is what I'm waiting for.'"

The cigarette holder balanced delicately between the fingers of one hand, the stem of a crystal wine glass pressed between the fingers of the other, Mother Russia shakes with laughter.

"Don't go away, there's more," Pravdin gasps. "When I say I'm waiting for the state to wither away, this old bat in front of me wags her gouty finger in my face and tells"— Pravdin can barely get the words out he is laughing so hard— "she tells me, *'Don't hold your breath!'*"

"Don't hold your breath," Mother Russia repeats, and she and Pravdin roar together.

Nadezhda stands at the kitchen door looking from one to the other, not quite sure what to make of it all. Silence reaches out from her like a hand and touches Pravdin; the sound of laughter slips away and then the muscular spasms of the laughter, and he is left gasping for breath, staring at the girl with the tangled sun-bleached hair plaited into two braids that meet and twine into one another at the nape of her neck. She is wearing a sleeveless blue sweater and blue jeans and a broad-brimmed straw hat with dried wild flowers tucked into a blue band. She enters the room with a flowing motion of broad hips on soft flat soundless shoes, deposits her net *avoska* full of onions on the table, embraces Mother Russia.

"Pravdin, Robespierre Isayevich," Pravdin declares, leaping to his feet and clicking together the heels of his sneakers, "at your beck and call. I'm the new attic."

Nadezhda takes a pad from her pocket, writes on the top page, tears it off and hands it to Pravdin. On it she has written:

"Oos, Nadezhda Victorovna. Hello to you."

"Hello back to you, little sister," Pravdin answers uneasily, glancing at Mother Russia, holding the scrap of paper in his hand.

A trace of a smile touches Nadezhda's lips. She nods, turns back to Zoya and excitedly taps her briefcase; she has come home with a treasure. She scribbles the details on her pad. "Enormous line, joined naturally, waited forty minutes, no idea what was for sale till I came near the head. Oh Zoya, see what I found."

Nadezhda pulls from her briefcase a large glossy book of Hieronymus Bosch reproductions. "Look for God's sake at this triptych," exclaims Mother Russia, turning the pages. "What a delicious discovery. Feel the paper. Oh my God, it's French or Swiss, absolutely no question about it. What did you pay?"

Nadezhda flashes ten fingers four times.

"Forty!" Pravdin marvels, his palm slapping against his forehead. "A steal is what it is. I can get you three times that with one phone call."

Nadezhda smiles and shakes her head, and Mother Russia says, "She would never sell such a thing."

Later, gathered around the table for dinner (lentil salad, fried mushrooms, an infusion made from red vine leaves), Mother Russia goes over her day for Nadezhda. "Another letter from Singer," she reports. "This one was signed by Mister Singer again. He's not interested in the photographs and claims I have to get an import license before he can send me the part I need." To Pravdin she explains: "Did you notice the old sewing machine in my room? It's been *hors de combat* ever since I had it almost. A darling little repairman figured out which piece was broken, and I've been trying to get the Singer Sewing Machine Company to send it to me."

Nadezhda scribbles, "Show the letters."

But Mother Russia waves away the suggestion impatiently. "They wouldn't interest him," she insists. "Ha! I'll tell you something funny about those Americans. I signed my first letter Volkova, Z.A., and Singer saluted me in his reply as 'Dear Sir.' Now I sign them 'Mother Russia.' But that's another story."

"Little mother, don't you get into trouble with all these letters?" asks Pravdin.

"What trouble?" she cries. "I've been certified." When Pravdin looks confused, she elaborates. "I've been certified *insane*. It happened right after the Great Patriotic War, in February of forty-six to be exact. I had been writing letters for years about my husband; he was killed in the camps in thirty-nine or forty." Mother Russia looks uncertainly at Nadezhda, who encourages her with a nod. "Yes, you see, it came about this way: there was a commission on some important matter and everyone voted yes except my husband, the lovely little idiot, who voted no. He knew what he was doing of course. Right after the vote he made his way back to our flat and packed a small bag with his toilet articles and some extra socks and underwear and books. I knew they would come for him that night because of the five black cats. I remember the footsteps, the knock at the door." Mother Russia smiles sadly. Nadezhda puts a hand on her arm and Zoya pats it. "I wrote letters all through the thirties trying to find out if he was alive. Just before the war started the packages I sent to him every month began coming back marked 'Deceased,' and for some reason only the bureaucrats know, 'No forwarding address.' Then I started writing letters to clear his name. I wrote to everyone: to local party people, to the newspapers, to the judges. I wrote to the great mountaineer—"

"*Waak, waak, rev-lutions are verbose,*" comes from the partly open door of Mother Russia's room.

"—the great mountaineer himself, and I even received an answer once, from what I supposed was a secretary, saying that Iosif Vissarionovich was occupied with the war and would get back to me when it was over. Well, he got back to me all right. They came to collect me in the middle of the night and carted me off to an asylum near Leningrad. I was there for three and a half years, and in a certain sense it was worth it. I can see that surprises you, doesn't it? You see, when they tossed me back into the lake they certified me insane, which more or less gives me license to do as I please, write what I please to whom I please. They can't touch me as long as I don't hurt anybody because I'm legally insane!"

Everyone is moved by the story: Mother Russia by the telling of it, Nadezhda and Pravdin by the listening to it. After a while Pravdin says, "I can guess those were hard years for you in the asylum."

"Oh, they were, I'll admit it, difficult," Mother Russia agrees. "The worst thing was the slamming of doors. I have a feeling that is threatening to become a theory: that the way you close doors shows in a profound sense what you think of the people inside. I imagine in the Kremlin they pad about on thick carpets and ease the doors closed so that you can't even hear the latch click into place. In my asylum the insane people who claimed to be doctors would fling the doors shut as if it were an afterthought. Slam! Like that." Mother Russia slaps the table and winces at the noise and the memory it evokes.

Pravdin begins to clear away the dishes. Nadezhda scrubs up and sets them to drain. Mother Russia turns in; she is planning to take an electric train into the countryside the next day to pick mushrooms and wants to get an early start.

"I'm pleased with our new attic," she whispers to Pravdin as she goes, and stretches on her toes to kiss him on each cheek.

Nadezhda invites Pravdin into her room for a nightcap. He settles awkwardly on the edge of the bed, which is covered with a quilt and embroidered pillows and serves as a couch. Nadezhda places an old Glenn Miller record on the phonograph, wipes it with a soft cloth, sets the needle in the first groove. She pours out two small cognacs, offers one to Pravdin. They click glasses and drink.

The room is lighted by a Japanese paper lantern in one corner. On a low table near the bed is a large basket full of dried flowers from Lenin Hills. Pravdin picks up one with a long stem and pale violet flowers, and Nadezhda writes on her pad: "Parnassia palustris."

The walls are covered with ornate gilt frames, several with old blown-up photographs of Civil War battle fields strewn with corpses, one with a map of the Paris Metro, some with nothing in them at all but wall. One series of photographs in particular catches Pravdin's eye: four stills that have captured, through streaks of light and a suggestion of blurring, the motion of the earth.

"Extraordinary is what they are," Pravdin comments. "Who made them?"

"I made them," writes Nadezhda. "I work as a photographer at the central fashion house. These I do for me."

Pravdin is mesmerized by the photographs. "The people

in these photos look as if they're being pulled in different directions by forces they can't control," he says. He shakes his head in admiration.

Nadezhda writes excitedly, "We are being pulled in different directions—we are in giddy motion. The earth's spin on its axis = 16 miles a minute. Around the sun = 1,200 miles a minute. Solar system moves through local star system = 780 miles a minute. Local star system moves through Milky Way = 12,000 miles a minute. Milky Way moves with respect to distant galaxies = 6,000 miles a minute. All in different directions!!!"

"We are being pulled apart, little sister. They are all in your photographs, every one of these motions. On display is where these should be."

"Not possible," Nadezhda quickly writes. "They say they don't present life as it really is. They say such photographs might be misinterpreted."

"They say, they say, they say," sneers Pravdin.

Nadezhda writes: "You sound as if you want to change the system."

"You've got it all wrong, little sister." Pravdin laughs. "All I want to do with the system is beat it."

"What do you do for work?" Nadezhda asks.

"For work I do what everyone does," Pravdin answers, "which is as little as possible. Actually, I'm what is known as a professional hustler."

"Hustler?"

"It's like this, little sister: When I was a boy I lived in a village not far from Moscow. Nowadays it's a watering hole for certain artists who know which side their bread is buttered on. In those days the local militia used to pay ten rubles to anyone bringing in a viper, which gave me the bright idea to breed them. I dug a snake pit behind the cottage and raised vipers, and once or twice a week I would make my way to the militia headquarters and hand in a dead snake and collect the bounty. I brought in so many that the regional paper wrote me up and the Komsomol pinned a medal on me. I lost that medal, but I still have the cottage; a teenage hustler breeds vipers in the same pit. Nothing is what changes."

Nadezhda writes: "I don't believe a word."

"True is what it is, little sister, all of it and more. Listen," he says, leaning forward, "what I do is buy and sell: blue jeans, records, automobile parts, residence permits, exit visas, electrical appliances, books, and so forth and so on. But I have big plans too." And he tells her about his idea for developing the Q-Tip and the classic comic.

"I have heard about such people as you," Nadezhda writes, "but I have never met one before. How do you stay out of the way of the police?"

"By giving them, from time to time, things that they need too," Pravdin explains. "Screening for a dacha, a carburetor for a 1956 Mercedes, tickets to a hockey match; I am famous in certain circles because I managed to acquire twelve tickets to the final with Canada last winter. At the time they had approximately the same value on the open market as exit visas to Israel."

"And so the police leave you alone."

"Up to now," Pravdin agrees. He remembers the microphone in his room. "Can I use that?" he asks. She hands him her pad. He writes:

"Before me who lived in the attic?"

"A Berber girl," Nadezhda writes her answer under the question, "with a blue flower tattooed on her cheek." Nadezhda looks at Pravdin quizzically, then scribbles: "Why do you write your question?"

"So that anyone listening will hear only the scratching of a pencil," he writes back.

CHAPTER 3

Pravdin, squinting
into the morning . . .

Pravdin, squinting into the morning so that the corners of
his eyes look like tiny fans, leans over the sill with the eucalyptus branch to see what the commotion is about.

"Sorry if we woke you, Comrade Eisenhower," calls
Ophelia Long Legs, looking up from scattering bread crumbs
to a flock of pigeons.

Pravdin closes the window, dresses, gulps down an obligatory cup of black coffee, ransacks the attic for his appointment
calendar, finds it under several copies of Solzhenitsyn's *First
Circle* in German, confirms the breakfast for the Lithuanian
physicist at the Metropole. He pulls on his Eisenhower jacket,
double knots the laces on his basketball sneakers, fills his

briefcase with Q-Tips and assorted odds and ends until it is bulging, starts downstairs. *Count your blessings,* Pravdin mumbles under his breath. *You're reasonably healthy, relatively wealthy and you live in the last wooden house in central Moscow. Touch wood.* (His knuckles rap on the banister.)

Ophelia sits on the bottom step of the porch, her long legs stretched out before her, absently chewing gum and contemplating the milling pigeons. "Which came first," she asks suddenly, "the Second World War or the Korean war?"

"The Second World War," Pravdin informs her. "Why are you asking such a question?"

"Oh, just like that." Ophelia shrugs. "I suppose you could say I'm naturally curious."

The screen door bangs behind them. Ophelia's first floor neighbor, Porfiry Yakolev, the weatherman with the handlebar mustache, steps briskly into the sunlight, takes several deep breaths.

"Pravdin, Robespierre Isayevich," Pravdin announces, "at your beck and call."

"Yakolev, Porfiry Osifovich," the weatherman returns the greeting. He shifts his umbrella and raincoat and briefcase to his left hand, shakes with Pravdin.

"Why all the rain gear?" Ophelia teases. "You predicted sunshine on television last night."

The weatherman casts a professional eye at the crystal sky, sniffs the air as if it is vintage wine, frowns. "Low front moving in from the east," he murmurs, "overcast by midafternoon with the possibility of scattered showers toward evening." He nods formally to Pravdin and hurries off down the alley.

Master Embalmer of the Soviet Union Yan Ernestovich Makusky emerges a few minutes later. He is a small, nervous old maid of a man who chews passionately on his cuticles in any kind of social situation. Pravdin creates one by introducing himself. Blinking anxiously, the master embalmer attacks the cuticles on one hand, shakes with the other. Pravdin's nostrils flare delicately; the odor of formaldehyde has reached his nose—or is it his imagination? He suddenly remembers what Ophelia whispered to him when he arrived: he is holding the hand that touches the clenched fist, combs the beard, *adjusts the facial expression* even of the Great Leader, the Living Light, Vladimir Ilyich himself. ("*Waak, help,*" echoes in Pravdin's head.) "Is it true, comrade embalmer," he demands urgently, drawing closer to Makusky, "that you are in personal charge of the body of our beloved Lenin?"

Makusky tugs until Pravdin is obliged to let go of his hand, brings a hangnail to his lips, acknowledges the fact with a downward jerk of his head.

"Tell me, if it's not a state secret, comrade embalmer," Pravdin urges, his lips almost against Makusky's ear. "Is it really Vladimir Ilyich there in the flesh, or a wax dummy?"

Makusky turns to stare at Pravdin with a hurt look in his eyes. Pravdin (sure now that the formaldehyde is not a figment of his imagination) backs off. "Consider the question withdrawn," he fumbles, smiling nervously.

"Lenin lives," the master embalmer spits through clenched lips, hefts his briefcase, darts off down the alley, scattering the pigeons in his path.

"What's itching him?" Ophelia wonders, throwing a handful of crumbs to the pigeons filtering back in twos and threes toward the porch in Makusky's wake.

General Shuvkin, crew cut and ramrod straight in a pressed three-piece civilian suit with the left sleeve doubled back and neatly pinned to the shoulder, struts onto the porch, gives a last-minute shine to his shoes by rubbing them on the back of his trousers. His eyes wander over Pravdin, take in his sneakers, the Eisenhower jacket (vaguely familiar) and come to a staring stop at the Order of Lenin dangling on his chest.

"Shuvkin," the general snaps, offering his only hand.

"Pravdin," Pravdin fires back. They shake once.

"Campaigns?" the general demands.

Pravdin permits his eyes to water at the thought of comrades dead and buried in far off fields. "Stalingrad under Chuikov, Belorussia under Cherniakhovsky, Berlin under Zhukov, comrade general."

The general nods knowingly; his lips purse; his mind's eye summons up row upon row of grave markers meandering like furrows in the caked Ukrainian earth. "My car's at the foot of the alley," Shuvkin orders. "I offer you a lift."

Waving to Ophelia, Pravdin falls into place on the general's left side, does a little jig to get into lock step with him. Shuvkin asks where he is going. Pravdin tells him about the breakfast for the Lithuanian physicist at the Metropole.

"So you are a physicist then," Shuvkin notes; he guessed that the eccentricity represents genius, not power.

"In a manner of speaking," Pravdin replies vaguely. His voice conveys that there are things one doesn't talk about, even with generals.

Shuvkin picks up the hint. "I understand completely," he says.

The general's orderly holds open the rear door of the shiny black Volga with shirred curtains on the windows and a discreet plastic flag with two stars on the right front fender. Pravdin, his corporal instinct surfacing, ducks and enters first, settles into a seat on the street side, fidgets (generals are not his cup of tea), brushes off the shoulders of his Eisenhower jacket specks that aren't there. The Volga pulls away from the curb. Through the front window Pravdin can see uniformed policemen flagging down cross traffic as soon as they catch sight of the general's two-star flag on the fender. To make conversation, Pravdin tells Shuvkin about an old idea of his (Hero of Socialist Labor! Order of the Red Star!! And so forth and so on) to publish an illustrated book of Red Army exercises. Reducing is an idea whose time has come, Pravdin begins. Warming to the subject, he goes on to spell out the advantages: Russian women will become slimmer and more attractive than their capitalist sisters; as women slim down they will require less room, thus alleviating the housing shortage; their stomachs will shrink, thus alleviating pressure on the agriculture sector of the economy and permitting the funneling of agriculture funds into military hardware. As the state withers away, Pravdin argues passionately, so too will the excess fat; Russia will become a trim muscular nation of builders of communism.

"Interesting," comments Shuvkin. "What was the reaction to your proposal?"

"An All-Union Sports functionary sipped carrot juice and listened politely," Pravdin recalls, "but decided he couldn't make a move without the approval of the Ministry of Defense. The Ministry of Defense people drank kvass from paper cups and concluded that anything that had to do with the Red Army, including its exercise programs, was classified information requiring Central Committee clearance. The Central Committee's second Directorate drank imported Scotch on the rocks in crystal glasses and said they couldn't proceed without the green light from GLAVLIT. The GLAVLIT people served lukewarm ersatz coffee and agreed the project had potential, but insisted that nothing could be done until it had been taken up with the All-Union Sports Directorate."

The Volga slides to a stop in front of a gray stone structure on Dzershinsky Square not far from the Kremlin. Almost instantly the orderly has the general's door open. Shuvkin steps onto the sidewalk, beckons his eccentric passenger to follow;

this is the end of the line and Pravdin finds himself bidding good day to the general before the main entrance to the KGB complex—a building he has studiously avoided even passing in front of before!

Retreating as nonchalantly as his pounding pulse will permit, Pravdin almost crashes into a sidewalk vendor demonstrating to silently watchful children tiny metal wind-up dolls doing military turns on the pavement. Pravdin's fingers close around his piece of chalk; his eyes search out a rectangle of gray wall on the KGB building. Various juicy phrases come to mind and he is mightily tempted, but at the crucial moment he senses a certain wobbliness in his legs, a weakness in his writing wrist; in short, a loss of nerve. He bends his head into a wind that isn't blowing and hurtles on.

Passing GUM department store across from Lenin's Tomb, Pravdin senses currents of strength flowing back into his veins. He pauses to tighten a sneaker lace, quickly scrawls on a ledge:

To dine with the devil use a long spoon

(Anon: Pravdin, even in the camps, had the instincts of a gourmet). Checking to be sure no one has spotted him defacing public property, he hurries off toward the Metropole.

"Pravdin, R. I.," Pravdin announced to the amazon with the guest list blocking the entrance, "at your beck and call."

She coolly checks the *P*'s, looks up at Pravdin, checks the *P*'s a second time, shakes her head sternly. "No Pravdin," she says with finality.

"Of course there's no Pravdin," Pravdin whispers. "Have you taken leave of your senses? Do you think they would permit my name to appear on a list that any Western operative could get his hands on. Reflect," Pravdin orders, tapping a forefinger against his skull. "Are you a member of the Party?"

The amazon nods carefully.

"Then it comes as no secret to you that we are surrounded by enemies, that vigilance is everybody's occupation." Pravdin makes sure nobody is within earshot, leans across the table. "If anyone inquires whether there is a Pravdin, R. I., at the breakfast, you will know what to say."

"You can count on me, comrade," the amazon pledges.

Pravdin rewards her with a crooked smile, brushes past her into the Metropole dining room. Just inside the door he comes across Friedemann T.

"Bitch, isn't she?" his old friend mutters, a coffee in one hand, a glass of slivovitz in the other. "What are we here? Literary?"

"What we are is theoretical physics," Pravdin informs him, plucking a glass of slivovitz from the bar.

"Theoretical physics." Friedemann T. takes this in, screws up his face as if he is flipping through some mental file cards, raises his voice. "Don't you agree that formulating the correct question is more difficult than trying to answer it?"

Pravdin captures a plate of scrambled eggs, uncaps a salt cellar, pours salt into his palm, sprinkles some of it over the eggs and throws the rest over his shoulder. "Einstein once told Max Planck," he casually remarks between mouthfuls of egg, "that it is the theory that decides what we observe."

"I have always marveled at the simplicity of Marx's response to Hume's problem of induction," ventures Friedemann T. He grabs two sugar buns from a passing tray and offers one to Pravdin. Across the room the Lithuanian physicist, a mousy man with green-gray skin, is uttering a few stock words of appreciation to his hosts. There is a smattering of applause when he finishes.

"I met him last time he had breakfast here," Pravdin recalls, motioning with his sugar bun toward the Lithuanian. "He suffers from the cult of the personality without the benefit of having a personality." Something occurs to him. "Perhaps that's why he only rates a breakfast."

"Lithuanian theoretical physics," Friedemann T. snickers, "is still trying to perfect the wheel."

As they leave Friedemann T. asks Pravdin how he made out with his apartment hunting. Pravdin, dislodging bits of food wedged between his teeth with a toothpick, tells him about the last wooden house in central Moscow and the odd vegetarian called Mother Russia.

"But she's quite famous," exclaims Friedemann T. His head rolls in wonder. "She's the crazy lady who is always writing letters to Brezhnev, whom she claims is the same little Leonid Ilyich she went to primary school with. Nobody believes her, of course, but the letters are sensational. Some of them were published in *samizdat* a year or so ago."

Friedemann T. stops in his tracks and stares at Pravdin; the goateed painter has put two and two together. "Now I understand," he mutters under his breath.

"Understand what?" Pravdin demands. "What understand?"

"It's probably because you're sharing an apartment with Mother Russia," Friedemann T. concludes. He throws an arm over Pravdin's shoulder and draws him off to a corner. "I must say, you had me worried. There have been whispers about you in the last day or so."

"What whispers?" Pravdin cries in an agonized voice.

"Not to get excited," Friedemann T. tries to calm Pravdin. "It's nothing you can put your finger on. Just, well, whispers. One gets the impression that you are being talked about in the wrong places."

"What talked about?" Pravdin's voice is a contained shriek. "What wrong places?"

"Pull yourself together," hisses Friedemann T. He looks around to see if anyone has taken notice of them. "It probably has to do with your moving in with a crazy lady who writes to Brezhnev, that's all. You must consider yourself lucky to have the apartment and forget about the rest."

"My cup runneth over," Pravdin moans, placing a hand to his cheek as if he is trying to dampen the throb of an aching tooth.

Pravdin is still edgy as he hurries to his midmorning appointment with the State Committee for Inventions and Discoveries. He jaywalks across an intersection without waiting for the light to turn, barely sets foot on the curb when a police whistle shrills almost behind his ear. Pravdin, out of his skin with fear, leaps a hundred and eighty degrees to find himself confronted by a grim-faced police officer with his arms folded across his impressive chest.

"Do you see the crosswalk markings over there?" demands the policeman.

"I have this appointment—"

"You have this appointment. Everyone always has this appointment. How old are you?"

"How old am I?" The question stuns Pravdin, if only because it is the last thing he expects to be asked. "You want to know how old I am? I'm forty-two is how old I am."

"At forty-two," the policeman lectures his captive jaywalker, "a citizen should know how to cross a street properly. Now turn around and go back and do it again the right way."

"Back again?" Pravdin stammers. "But if it's dangerous to jaywalk in this direction, it's dangerous to jaywalk back in the other direction!"

The policeman's eyes narrow. Without another word Pravdin jaywalks back through the traffic, returns on the crosswalk and continues on his way. Inside the ministry he waits his turn at the information desk. Nearby a heavy girl inserts a kopeck in a public scale and steps on. Four or five boys with long hair and leather jackets gather around her and begin to call off the numbers as the needle climbs. "Sixty, seventy, seventy-seven." The back of the girl's neck turns red; fighting tears, she thrusts through the semicircle of boys and disappears out the main door.

"Next," calls the woman behind the information counter.

"If you please, kind lady, the State Committee for Discoveries and Inventions is what I'm looking for," Pravdin informs her.

The woman, a timeserver with an eye tic, studies her directory. "No such animal," she drones. "Next."

Pravdin holds off the man behind him with his briefcase. "What do you mean, no such animal? I know for a fact that such an animal is what there is. Do me the favor of looking again. State Committee for Inventions and Discoveries."

"You said *Discoveries* and *Inventions*," the timeserver complains. She appeals to the others on the line. "He said *Discoveries* and *Inventions*. Make up your mind."

"Inventions and Discoveries, Discoveries and Inventions, what's the difference?" Pravdin cries hysterically.

The woman addresses herself to the people behind Pravdin. "There's a big difference, as any idiot could tell you. Discoveries and Inventions would be listed under *D*. Inventions and Discoveries would be listed under *I*." She shakes her head in disgust, slowly looks down again at the directory. "Inventions and Discoveries, State Committee of, third floor, five-oh-eight. Next."

Pravdin presents himself to a young male secretary posted just inside the door of five-oh-eight. "Pravdin, Robespierre Isayevich," he says. A number of men, all with small packages or contraptions on their laps, turn to look at the newcomer. Pravdin leans across the desk and lowers his voice. "It's about my idea for a cotton-tipped toothpick," he tells the male secretary.

"Meetings with the State Committee for Inventions and Discoveries are by appointment only," the male secretary explains earnestly. "You must write for an appointment."

"An appointment is what I already have," insists Pravdin. He rummages in his briefcase and produces a letter with the committee's letterhead. "Ten-thirty, see for yourself?"

The male secretary waves Pravdin to a vacant place on the bench between a man with an apple corer-peeler-and-slicer and another with an indestructible light bulb that he claims stores up sunlight during the day and plays it back at night. When Pravdin's turn comes, two hours behind schedule, he is ushered into a conference room where seven men and a woman sit around a table covered with green felt. They are spooning yogurts.

"You have five minutes," the woman informs him.

"My Q-Tip," Pravdin launches into his pitch, removing a box from his briefcase, pushing out with his primitively long thumb the cardboard drawer, offering one to the first man on his right as if it is a cigarette, "will revolutionize Russia. Before you can build communism you must construct socialism. Before socialism, an advanced industrial society. And who ever heard of an advanced industrial society without Q-Tips!"

"What did they say?" Nadezhda scrawls, hands Pravdin the slip of paper. (His trouser pockets are filled with crumpled notes; they have been talking for a while.)

"They ate yogurts and passed a Q-Tip from one to the other as if it would bite them and told me to take the matter up with the All-Union Institute for Household Technology."

They are huddled under a tree on Lenin Hills, which slopes up from the Moscow River and hovers over the city like the lid of an eye, waiting for the sun to burn through the shower. Water vapor rises from gravel paths. At a nearby tree a couple, their heads shielded under a copy of Pravda, is glued together in an embrace. An old peasant squats with his back to another tree sprinkling salt from a cellar onto scallions and biting off the tips. From excursion boats passing in the river below, the voices of guides on loudspeakers drift up through the trees.

"Look left, look right," Pravdin mimics. "What the tourists don't see is Moscow."

Nadezhda, in a sleeveless summer blouse, shivers and Pravdin drapes his Eisenhower jacket over her shoulders. They stand close to each other without touching. Nadezhda writes on a slip of paper:

"Zoya says you were in the camps."

Pravdin's crooked smile, a muscular contortion devoid of mirth, spreads across his face. "Twelve years I was in the camps," he confirms. Instinctively he glances at the couple under the newspaper, but they are absorbed with each other. "Nine of them in Siberia. I was arrested in the month of Ab in the year of our Lord five thousand seven hundred six." Pravdin smirks. "That's nineteen forty-five in Christian."

"Are you religious?" Nadezhda asks.

"Religious?" Pravdin jeers. "Me, I have no spiritual equipment."

"Why were you arrested?" writes Nadezhda.

"Why is what I never found out, little sister," Pravdin replies. "I was selling watches I took from Germans, but everyone was selling watches they took from Germans. It got so it was hard to find a German who knew the time of day. Nobody ever bothered to tell me why I had been arrested.

A trial I never had. An officer with blue shoulder boards read through my dossier and announced 'Eight years.' Count your blessings, I told myself, he could have easily said eighty."

"But you said twelve years," Nadezhda writes.

"Twelve is what his eight turned out to be, little sister. When I found myself alive at the end of eight, I presented my cold body at the desk of the commandant, a man who later died of hiccups, or so I heard. He looked up my dossier and announced I had been given a bonus of four more."

"How did you survive?" Nadezhda writes furiously.

"How I survived," Pravdin explains, "was by getting my hands on something that everyone in the camp wanted. I served most of my time at a place called Krivoshchekovo. The winters were so bitter you couldn't expose raw skin for more than a few seconds without getting frostbite. Fingers fell off if you lost a mitten. I told them I had been a nurse in the army and wangled a job in the medical section. There I got my hands on the list of female prisoners who had venereal disease. Every day dozens of people—prisoners, guards, brigade commanders, stoolies, cooks—would come to me and I would rent them the list for two minutes. They paid me in fistfuls of bread and spoonfuls of soup and cupfuls of tobacco and squares of cloth and stubs of pencils and scraps of metal and lengths of string. I was something of a celebrity in Krivoshchekovo for working out the official exchange rate. Four fistfuls of bread were equal to one bowl of soup were equal to eight grams of tobacco were equal to enough cloth to wind around an average foot were equal to—"

Nadezhda touches Pravdin's cheek with her fingertips; tears moisten her eyes.

Pravdin stops talking.

The rain lets up and Nadezhda backs away from the tree to photograph Pravdin with her old Leica. On an impulse she kicks off her sandals and scampers up the hill, slipping on the wet grass. Pravdin, picking his way around patches of mud, follows. Half way up they find a bench and sit on plastic bags that Pravdin produces from his briefcase. Nadezhda dips into her net sack and comes up with two oranges. She breaks the skin of hers with her teeth and peels it with her fingers, which are long and delicate. Pravdin fishes a knife from his pocket and attacks his. When the oranges are finished Pravdin throws the peels in a trash basket and Nadezhda takes out some chocolate cake and a carton of milk. She bites off the corner of the carton and drinks in gulps with her head thrown back.

The rain has given way to moist sunshine. Below and to the right some middle-aged women strip to their underwear to take the sun. "I heard once about the wife of one of our diplomats in New York who took off her clothes in a park and sunned herself in her underwear, as our women here do," Pravdin recounts. "Somehow her picture turned up in a newspaper and there was a great scandal. The Party members at the embassy got together to try her. She pleaded that her underwear were her best clothes—and got off!"

A black cat, its hair slick from the rain, wanders by, pauses to rub against Pravdin's trouser leg. Pravdin takes it as an omen but Nadezhda smiles, reaches down to touch its fur, then writes to Pravdin: "How very intelligent of it to be all black."

A blond boy wearing an embroidered Cossack shirt passes on the gravel path behind the bench. "Such a beautiful shirt," Nadezhda writes. "My grandfather used to wear such shirts."

"You like it?" Pravdin demands. "Ho, comrade, for how much do you sell your shirt?"

The boy shakes his head. "I don't sell it," he replies seriously, "but I'll trade it."

"Trade it is a good idea," Pravdin exclaims, pulling several Swiss watches from his briefcase. "For one of these you'll have to throw in some cash."

"I'll trade my shirt for her shirt," the boy grins.

Pravdin looks from one to the other in confusion but Nadezhda understands instantly. Leaping from the bench she strips off her shirt and holds it out to the boy. He studies her small pointed breasts for a delicious moment, then pulls his peasant shirt over his head and exchanges with her.

Nadezhda pulls on the embroidered shirt, which is much too big for her, and starts to roll up the sleeves. Pravdin turns away, red faced. The boy walks off with her shirt folded under his arm singing, "Why do girls like handsome boys?"

Climbing the narrow steel steps that lead to the top of the hill, Nadezhda asks Pravdin if he likes her new shirt.

"It is reasonably ugly," he answers, still in a bad humor.

"How can something be reasonable and ugly?" she asks.

"It is a play on words."

"You must not play with words," she writes. "They are serious things, words."

At the top Nadezhda rinses her feet in some clear rain puddles and dries them with a scarf, hoists herself up on the low wall to sit in the sun. Lomonosov University towers behind them, Moscow is spread out like a buffet before them: the thin needle of the TV tower, the Kremlin with the river twined around it like a vine, several Stalin gothics. Just across the river a soccer game is in progress in a giant bowl of a stadium, and every now and then a roar from the crowd drifts over the river.

"Explain if you can," Nadezhda writes, "why it is you live the way you live?"

"I live the way I do, little sister, in order to live."

Nadezhda dismisses the answer with an annoyed shake of her head.

Pravdin tries again. "When I came out of the camps, an old man of thirty-one is what I was. I had no skill, no profession; all I had was a notation in my workbook that I had served time, and another notation on my internal passport that I was Jewish. Between the two who would give me a job? Nobody would give me a job is who. So I threw away my workbook and became self-employed. The only way I could live was inside the Jewish cliché—as a hustler on the make. As long as I do what everyone expects me to do, I am left to my own devices. I also have a theory, if you want to know it, that I fulfill a very important function in our socialist paradise. I supply people who have money with something to spend it on."

"You make yourself sound important," Nadezhda notes on her pad.

"Important is what I am," Pravdin says sourly. "I take from the rich and give to me." And he bends down and scrawls in chalk along the sidewalk under Nadezhda's feet:

Behind every fortune is a crime

(H. de Balzac: Pravdin once spent two months in solitary with a Balzac nut).

Nadezhda winds the sandal straps around her ankles, ties them, starts walking toward the Metro station.

"Thank you," she jots on a slip that she offers to Pravdin.

Still annoyed about the exchange of shirts, he crumples the note without reading it. "How could you do such a thing?" he demands, tugging at the rolled-up sleeve of her embroidered shirt.

She presses another note into his hand. It says:

"Who was hurt?"

CHAPTER 4

I know what
we are here . . .

"I know what we are here," boasts Friedemann T., helping himself to a generous portion of caviar from the sideboard.

"How could you not know," remarks Pravdin, gesturing with his caviar and toast toward the chess players. A flamboyant Russian grand master named Zaitsev is strutting back and forth between two long tables full of very serious blue-blazered members of a British chess club. Zaitsev, who is playing twelve games simultaneously, grips a chesspiece in his fist and slams it down on the board with a roar.

"He never had a chance," he tells the crowd of onlookers. "If God played the Benoni against God, white would win!"

Zaitsev reaches across the table to accept a glass of champagne, drinks off half of it in one smooth swallow, struts on to the next board. He tilts his great head and examines it for a moment, then pounces on a piece. "Check! Tell the truth—you didn't anticipate that, did you? Never mind, you're in good company: I crushed Petrosian in the sixty-nine interzonals with the same move."

Zaitsev sails on to the next board, which is opposite Friedemann T. and Pravdin. He studies the position for a long moment with a baffled expression. Suddenly his eyes surge open as he spots the flaw in his opponent's game. "But you haven't done your homework," he taunts. "Fischer tried pawn queen five in a queen's gambit declined in fifty-nine and lost eighteen moves later!"

"That's new," Friedemann T. comments loudly. "He's accepting an isolated pawn in return for a king's side attack."

"The poisoned pawn variation of the Najdorf defense is Zaitsev's specialty," Pravdin notes. He takes another bite of toast and caviar, sips champagne, adds:

"The offered pawn is what he always accepts."

"I don't really like caviar," Friedemann T. admits on their way out of the chess club. "I don't appreciate all those little explosions in my mouth."

"I don't mind the caviar," Pravdin confesses, "but vodka I prefer to champagne any day. A headache is what champagne always gives me."

Friedemann T. pauses to look in a department store window. "I don't mean to alarm you," he says quietly, "but one of us is being followed."

"What followed?" Pravdin cries nervously. "Where followed?"

"The tall man in the blue raincoat at the kiosk. We'll split up at the corner and see which one of us is the pigeon."

They separate, walking off in different directions. When

they are half a block apart Friedemann T. turns and points at Pravdin as if to say, "It's you."

Pravdin, cursing under his breath, dashes down a side street, turns up an alley behind a theater, pauses to scrawl on the wall:

Full conformity is possible only in the cemetery

(I. Stalin: Pravdin has tried to grin and bear it), hears footsteps behind him and hurries on. Minutes later he pushes through the front door of GUM, the giant department store across Red Square from the Kremlin, plunges into the crowd and drifts with its flow. At a men's clothing stall he ducks into a fitting room, watches through a slit in the curtain as the man in the blue raincoat, angrily looking right and left, rushes by. Pravdin hurtles back the way he came, dives into the Metro and emerges into the sunlight at the stop nearest the Hotel Ukraine, where he waits to see if Blue Raincoat is still behind him.

He isn't.

Pravdin hurries off down Kutuzovsky Prospect to keep his rendezvous with the American journalist. He meets him in a coffee shop one flight up. Pravdin picks up a black coffee and a bun at the counter and joins the journalist, whose name is Hull, at a table. They don't speak until they are alone.

"Coming here I was followed," Pravdin blurts out.

"Maybe they picked up on you when you phoned the office," Hull, a hulking, balding man with feverish eyes, tells Pravdin.

"Not possible," Pravdin assures him. "I phoned from a pay booth and neither of us mentioned my name."

The journalist shrugs. "If they were going to haul you in, they would have done it a long time ago. What about the interview with the kids who use drugs?"

"What about my fee?" Pravdin retorts.

Hull hands him an envelope, Pravdin stuffs it into his briefcase and gives the journalist a slip of paper with an address and a time written on it. "They will be watching to see if you are followed," he reminds him. "If you are, they won't be around when you get there. The conditions you understand? In your article, no names and fifty rubles a head for them."

Hull nods. "Listen, Pravdin, there's a choreographer with the Bolshoi who is supposed to have lost his job for applying for an exit visa to Israel. I don't have a name but maybe you could nose around and set up something for me."

"Maybe," Pravdin says evasively.

"I also hear—" A lame lady limps by and Hull waits for her to pass. "I hear there's a story in you."

Pravdin spits a mouthful of coffee back into his cup. "What story where in me?" he wails. "Where do you hear such things?"

An army officer puts his coffee and bun on their table and goes off in search of a chair.

"I heard it from a Swedish correspondent, who says he got it from someone called the Druse. Does the name mean anything to you?"

"The Druse," Pravdin protests sullenly, fighting down hysteria, "is no one I ever heard of."

Pravdin, a maître d' from a seedy hotel, ducks in and out of the milling crowd, a bottle of mineral water in one hand, in the other a vinegary Georgian red ("Ha!" sneers Zoya, "*mis en bouteille dans le sous-sol de GUM*") filling with delicate flicks of his thin wrist and a terminal flourish the half-empty glasses of the guests.

"The trouble with Russia," Zoya is lecturing some of her friends, "is that she kills her artists."

"America kills them too," Pravdin stage whispers, splashing wine into her outstretched glass, "by making them rich."

"Zoya, dear, wherever did you find him?" cried Ludmila Serafimovna, one of Mother Russia's cronies who lives in the prewar apartment building that backs onto the alley. "He's absolutely adorable. In those funny shoes one can't even hear him coming up on one."

"I didn't find him," Zoya explains cheerfully. "He's our new attic."

"*Quelle chance*," Ludmila Serafimovna exclaims. "Ah, there she is, the birthday girl herself," and she cuts through the crowd like the prow of a ship, silk scarfs trailing from her fingertips, to embrace Nadezhda.

"Wine or water?" Pravdin offers Friedemann T., who has backed a very drunk General Shuvkin into a corner and blocks his escape with his caped body.

"The reason socialist realism doesn't move people," Friedemann T. is saying—"wine," he flings at Pravdin and holds out his glass for a refill—"is that it shows them as they are. Take it from someone who has an instinct for such matters, the only thing that catches the attention of people is to show them, even for a fleeting moment, what they could become. This is the point of departure for my abstract socialist realism, you see."

"Campaigns?" hiccups the general.

"I beg your pardon?" Friedemann T. inquires in confusion.

"*Waak, waak, help, help.*" A flutter of wings! Vladimir Ilyich, somehow loose from his cage, sails around the room, winds up perched on Mother Russia's broken Singer.

"Isn't he beautiful," squeals Ophelia Long Legs. "Look, comrade Eisenhower, a genuine bird!" She holds out her wine glass to Vladimir Ilyich; frightened by all the attention, he backs off, wings beating the air, then leaps to the curtain rod above the window, out of arm's reach.

"Help, waak, help, waak."

"All the same," Porfiry Yakolev, the weatherman with the handlebar mustache, is telling a group, "everybody should have a hero. Lenin perhaps. Or Marx. Or Engels. Something to give you a standard against which to measure your own performance."

"My hero," Zoya says sweetly, "is that darling little misfit Voltaire."

"I don't believe I know the name," ventures Master Embalmer Yan Makusky.

"The Frenchman Voltaire," Mother Russia explains. "He had to struggle with pain every single day of his life. But he produced more work than any other ape on this planet, with the possible exception of an agrarian reformer named Mao Tse-tung. You have heard of Mao Tse-tung, I take it? Unlike Mao, Voltaire led an active social life while he was doing all this. And I might add," she says with a wink, "an active sexual life."

"Ah." The weatherman's mouth falls open. His fingers twist the tip of his mustache into a point. "Sexual life, you say?"

"Nowadays our insane hyenas of psychiatry, those pimply führers in white coats, devote whole books trying to define that superior genital love-object, but my darling Voltaire did it in one neat sentence when he wrote his ugly little niece, 'Both my heart and my prick love you!' "

Porfiry Yakolev almost chokes on his mineral water and Mother Russia has to pound him on the back to help him over the crisis.

Threading the brim of a fedora nervously through his fingers, Master Embalmer Makusky notes, "You seem to know a great deal about psychiatry. Do you have a background in the discipline?"

"In a manner of speaking," Zoya allows. "I was diagnosed paranoid schizophrenic by a malevolent ass when I was a textbook example of what schizophrenia and paranoia are not: warm, loving, outgoing, uninhibited, funny, sexy, bawdy, lively, happy and life-loving."

"In a word," the weatherman, recovered from his coughing fit, offers, "you were innocent."

"*Waak, help.*" Vladimir Ilyich lifts on his claws, beats at the air with his wings, settles back onto the curtain rod.

"In our epoch," snaps Mother Russia, "innocence is no longer pertinent. But that's another story."

Mother Russia hooks her arm through Ludmila Serafimovna's and pulls her into a corner. "I sent off another zinger to Singer today," she confides in her friend. "My fingers are swollen from typing the copies-to. I don't know how long he'll be able to hold out against me."

"I wouldn't want to be in his shoes." Ludmila Serafimovna laughs. The two women giggle conspiratorially, and Zoya's friend demands: "What did you hit him with this time?"

"I told him," Zoya boasts triumphantly, "that Singer ruined sewing."

"Oh dear," Ludmila Serafimovna cries excitedly, "that should give him something to think about."

Ophelia Long Legs switches off the naked overhead bulb just as Pravdin emerges from the kitchen carrying a birthday cake with lighted candles. The guests cluster around Nadezhda, whose eyes sparkle in the candlelight. Ludmila Serafimovna counts the candles. "Twenty-four, twenty-five, twenty-six—but my dear, you don't look a day over nineteen!"

"She looks young," Pravdin mutters, "but she talks old."

Nadezhda takes a deep breath and blows out all the candles but one. Pravdin moistens his primitively long, broken, badly set thumb and his forefinger and extinguishes the last flame between them.

"Leave everything," Mother Russia instructs Pravdin. "We'll clean up tomorrow. I enjoyed your friend Friedemann T. What does he do for a living?"

"Anything," replies Pravdin.

"Not funny," groans Zoya.

"Not meant to be," says Pravdin.

"Dear Robespierre, you look like a man of the world." Zoya drops into a seat across the kitchen table from Pravdin. "I need some advice on how one goes about getting an import license."

"What don't we manufacture in this socialist paradise that you need an import license for?" Pravdin wants to know.

"I need a piece for my Singer sewing machine, and the only—"

Nadezhda hands Zoya a note. "Come help with the birthday presents."

"Think about it," Zoya orders Pravdin. The two of them follow Nadezhda into her room and watch as she attacks the boxes piled on her bed.

"How nice of the general," exclaims Mother Russia as Nadezhda peels away paper from a Czechoslovak hair dryer. Ophelia Long Legs has given her a pair of handmade leather sandals; Porfiry Yakolev, the weatherman, an alarm clock that wakes you up with the first notes of the "Internationale"; Yan Makusky, the embalmer, a recording of Uzbeki folk songs. Mother Russia's gift is wrapped in tissue paper. It is a small icon, faded with age, depicting the Virgin Mary and a very chubby infant Jesus. Nadezhda stares at it for a long moment, turns to Zoya and embraces her.

Pravdin fetches his present from the attic, self-consciously presents it to Nadezhda. "It is the best I could do, little sister, on such short notice," he apologizes.

Zoya gasps as Nadezhda removes the paper. "It is something people don't part with for money," she says in wonder.

Nadezhda runs her fingertips over Pravdin's gift as if she is blind and her impressions come from her sense of touch. It is an extremely rare volume of Mandelstam's collected poems published in 1928 and called simply, *Poems*. Three-quarters of the way through the book a small dried flower has been placed as a marker. Nadezhda opens to it immediately, reads the poem, hands the book to Zoya, who reads it aloud in a hoarse voice.

> . . . *your spine has been smashed forever,*
> *My beautiful, pitiful age,*
> *And with an inane, bewildered grimace*
> *You now look back, both cruel and weak*
> *At the tracks of your own paws.*

Mother Russia looks up. "Tell us how it is you found this book?" she asks in awe.

"You forget, little mother, that I am a hustler," replies Pravdin.

"You are to hustling," Zoya dismisses his answer impatiently, "as a sailor who is uncomfortable with the wind is to sailing."

They are reading some of the other poems, passing the book from one to the other, when Ophelia Long Legs comes bounding up the stairs carrying a small wooden trunk. "The attic before Comrade Eisenhower left this for Nadezhda," she explains breathlessly. "You remember, the one with the funny blue flower tattooed on her cheek. I asked her to come up but she dropped the trunk into my arms and raced off down the alley. I suppose," Ophelia says as she hands the trunk to Nadezhda, "she's shy is what it is. Say, what a neat record—can I borrow it?" Nadezhda nods and Ophelia hurries off downstairs with the Uzbeki folk songs.

"Here's a mystery," Mother Russia announces, obviously relishing the possibility.

Nadezhda bangs on the lock with the flat of her palm but it doesn't give. Pravdin opens the small blade of his pocket-knife and, kneeling with his eye almost against the wood, inserts it in the lock.

"There are parts of you we haven't been to yet," teases Zoya.

"Opening closed doors is my specialty," Pravdin says, delicately twisting the blade. Suddenly the lock snaps open. He lifts back the lid.

"Papers only," he says, disappointed.

"Manuscripts," Mother Russia corrects. She and Nadezhda exchange looks.

Nadezhda takes out the manuscripts, which are bound with faded red ribbons, and spreads them on the bed. The paper, thin and brown and brittle, is cracking with age. The writing has all been done in longhand. Nadezhda gently picks up a page, reads it, bursts into silent sobs.

Her voice reduced to a moan, Zoya quickly crosses herself and says: "Such things are not possible."

"What's going on?" cried Pravdin.

By now Mother Russia is reading and weeping too. The sight of the two women with tears streaming down their cheeks demoralizes Pravdin. He charges out of the room, slamming the door behind him, splashes water into the teapot and bangs it down on the stove. An instant later he pushes open the door of Nadezhda's room again. "No matches," he barks.

Nadezhda, drying her eyes on her sleeve, comes out and finds them for him. She gestures him aside and prepares three cups of camomile infusion, which she carries back into her room on a tray. Mother Russia, her eyes dry but red, is avidly skimming manuscript pages.

Pravdin pushes a lump of sugar into his mouth and noisily strains his infusion through it. The act of drinking something warm seems to calm everyone down considerably.

"And so?" Pravdin demands almost belligerently.

"I'll explain everything," Zoya promises, turning page after page of manuscript. She shakes her head as if the motion will clear it. "It is a miracle," she begins, "there is no other way to describe what has happened."

"You can describe what has happened," Pravdin remarks impatiently, "by describing what has happened."

Zoya nods, collects her thoughts. "Where to start? The story begins with a Cossack novelist named Krukov, who served with the Whites during the Civil War. In 1922 I think it was, he was wounded and spent the next fourteen months convalescing on the estate of an uncle. During those fourteen months he was known to have written the rough draft of a long novel on the Civil War called *The Deep Don*. In 1923 the Red Guards finally brought the Cossacks to heel, arresting and summarily executing the White officers they got their greasy little paws on. Krukov made no attempt to escape; there is a story that he put on his uniform and sword and went out to meet the Reds when they arrived. At any rate, he was interrogated by a young Komsomol activist known only as Filipovich. When members of Krukov's family attempted to find out what had happened to him, they learned that he had been put up against a wall and shot and that his manuscripts, which he kept in a small wooden trunk, had vanished."

Pravdin stares at the trunk on the floor.

"Four years later," Zoya continues, "a talentless short story hack named Ivan Filopovich Frolov—"

"*Frolov* is the Filopovich of your story!" Pravdin interrupts.

"Frolov published his epic, which he also called *The
Deep Don.*" Pravdin starts to interrupt again but she motions
him to wait. "Be patient; there is, God help us all, more.
The book, a sizzling masterpiece full of passionate characters
and breathtaking imagery, won for Frolov instant fame and
fortune. But there were whispers of plagiarism, and two or
three articles found their way into the newspapers abroad. To
clear the air the Bolsheviks organized a commission in 1929
to investigate the situation and report on who was the real
author of *The Deep Don.* The committee consisted of four
writers and four editors, all members of the Party, to be sure."

"To be sure," echoes Pravdin.

"The matter seemed to be open and shut. Frolov was
unable to produce his original manuscripts; he claimed they
had been lost in the war. His only contact with Cossacks and
Cossack life was his relatively short stint as a Red Army
interrogator, though he denied ever meeting a Cossack
named Krukov; his few short stories that had been published
showed no hint of the brilliance or imagery that mark every
page of *The Deep Don.* Krukov, on the other hand, had
lived among the Cossacks all his life. Unlike Frolov, he had
personally taken part in all the battles described in the novel.
And his published works made it obvious that he was more
likely to be the author of *The Deep Don* than the young
pretender Frolov. The only thing against Krukov was that
his manuscripts had disappeared during the war too—shortly
after his interrogation by the Komsomol activist Filopovich!
That's where matters stood when the Commission counted
noses. The result surprised no one: seven to one to uphold
Frolov's claim of authorship."

"And the eighth?" asks Pravdin.

"Ah, the eighth. The eighth member, a gentle editor of

children's books, was arrested and packed off to the camps, where he eventually gave up, as the saying goes, the ghost. Frolov, damn his soul, went on to win the Nobel Prize for Literature. And to publish other books. But none of them were ever on the same level as *The Deep Don.*"

Sapped of strength, Zoya sinks back into the cushions with a shudder.

"The eighth member of the commission," Pravdin puts the pieces of the puzzle together, "was your late lamented husband, the one who died in the camps."

"And Krukov," Zoya adds, "was Nadezhda's grandfather."

Pravdin winces, reaches instinctively for Nadezhda's hand. She lets him take it, leans down and touches her eyes, which are moist, to the back of his wrist.

Mother Russia snatches a page of manuscript. "Lies are like a sweater with a loose end," she cries passionately. "Pull and the whole thing unravels."

"That's exactly the problem," agrees Pravdin, leaping from the bed and pacing nervously around the room. "If they let you set this matter straight, there will be other clowns with the same idea." Pravdin gestures despairingly toward the alley, the city, the country. "The whole thing will unravel!"

"Robespierre is right," Nadezhda writes quickly, "we must move cautiously."

"By all means let us move cautiously," Zoya urges in a whisper, "but let us move."

Pravdin, holding his temple to contain the hot flashes of panic, groans. "What is this us? What disaster are you dragging me into?"

Zoya's eyes glisten with excitement. "Don't you see it," she demands. "*You were put here to help us.* Nadezhda can't talk. And nobody will listen to me because I've been certified. Which leaves you. With these manuscripts you will show up that usurper Frolov. You will vindicate my husband, God rest his silly soul. You will restore the reputation of Nadezhda's grandfather."

Pravdin's proscenium inclinations get the best of him. "I can see it now," he cries, shielding his eyes with his hand and squinting into a nonexistent spotlight stabbing down from a nonexistent balcony, "Robespierre Isayevich Pravdin. Hero of Socialist Labor! The Order of the Red Star!! The Order of the Red Banner!!! The Order of Lenin even!!!!"

Zoya flings her thin arms around Pravdin's neck. "You can't fail. Remember what Pasternak said about the irresistible power of unarmed truth." She taps the manuscripts triumphantly. "*Voilà*—here is unarmed truth!"

"Touch wood," Pravdin moans, reaching over and rapping his knuckles on the trunk. "How irresistible unarmed anything is is what we'll see."

Pravdin, an avenging Isaiah in flowing Bedouin robes, slumps between the humps of an animal he is afraid to identify, levels his cotton-tipped lance and charges the KGB building on Dzerzhinsky Square. Life-sized wind-up soldiers buzz around him like horse flies. Pravdin dips his lance into a bucket full of water lily root infusion and scrawls in invisible ink on the gray wall:

The revolution is incapable of regretting
(I. Stalin: Pravdin has read it and wept). The giant doors of the KGB building yawn open; the Druse, holding a guest list, bars the way. Blood trickles from his severed jugular. "Pravdin, R. I.," Pravdin calls out, "at your beck and call." The Druse shakes his head without looking at the list. "There is no Pravdin, R. I.," he says politely. A bird perches on Pravdin's head, squawks, "*Rev-lutions are verbose, waak, waak.*" "There is no Trotsky, L. D., either," insists the Druse. Pravdin flashes the crooked smile that signals he is about to gate-

crash, digs his spurs into the side of the beast he is afraid to identify. It rears back, empties its bowels with a spasmodic heave of its sphincter muscle. The aroma, reminiscent of sour mustard, burns Pravdin's nostrils, stings his eyes. He panics, fumbles frantically for his gas mask, comes up with only a handful of brittle pages bound in ribbons.

"Aiiiiiiiii!" screams Pravdin, bolting upright in bed, sweaty and weak and wide awake.

"Robespierre Isayevich," Mother Russia calls up from the bottom of the stairs leading to the attic. "Pssssssst, Robespierre Isayevich, are you, God forbid, ill?"

"Bad dreams," Pravdin responds, mopping the sweat on his forehead with his pajama sleeve.

"Come down then," Zoya orders. "I couldn't unfortunately sleep either. I'm brewing up a pot that will put the both of us out of our misery."

Pravdin folds an old robe around his bones, slips his feet into his sneakers without bothering to tie the laces, descends to the kitchen. Zoya, wearing an Uzbek robe and her fox furs, places two steaming cups on the table.

"An infusion won't help," complains Pravdin.

"This one will; it's three parts rum, one part boiling water, also sugar," Zoya reassures him. "*Nastrovia.*"

"*L'Chaim.*" Pravdin blows into his cup to cool it, sips noisily. "Zoya Aleksandrovna," he confesses, "there is something in all this business I can't put my thumb on."

"Try."

"Excuse me?"

"I said, try," Zoya repeats, a mischievous glint in her eyes. "Commence with the Druse."

Pravdin's voice slips several sprockets. "How do you know about the Druse?" he demands.

"I told you when you arrived that we would the both of us together try and figure out why you had come," Zoya

explains patiently. "The Druse, Chuvash Al-hakim bi'amrillahi, with his long pinky nail that indicates a taste for the ab-
surd, is the key."

Pravdin's eyes bulge. Questions stick at the back of his
throat like bones. Zoya enjoys his discomfort. "Four years ago
I was evicted from my room in Proletarsky when one of my
letters to Comrade Brezhnev wound up in the *New York
Times*. The thing that was unusual about this was I never
sent the letter to the *New York Times*. But that's another
story. I was desperate, you can imagine. I tried everything I
could think of to find a place to live. Nothing seemed to work.
Every time I came across something I liked, the papers would
mysteriously turn up indicating the apartment had already
been assigned to someone else. It was almost as if a ghost
were following me around and ruining my possibilities. I took
to looking over my shoulder, I was that upset. One day a man
on line behind me at the Housing Ministry whispered something about a Druse. I went to see him naturally; I was willing to try anything. He had nails that grew into the flesh at
the sides, an indication of luxurious tastes. And of course
there was his pinky nail. We drank a wonderful infusion
made from rose hips and *hell* and talked about reincarnation
and visits from other civilizations. Finally he asked me, almost as an afterthought, why I had come. I told him I needed
an apartment. He wrote a name and phone number on a
scrap of paper. When I called the number a man told me I
could have this"—Zoya indicates the door to her room. "So
here I am, in the last wooden house in central Moscow."

Pravdin stares at the shimmering images in his grog.
"Was Nadezhda here?" he asks.

"The general was here, along with Ophelia Long Legs and
the crew downstairs," Zoya says, "but the only person upstairs
was a strange young creature with a blue flower tattooed on
her cheek. She slept in the attic when she was here, which

wasn't very often; she would disappear for weeks at a time. She never received mail or phone calls, and only spoke to ask if there was anything she could pick up for me. The first time she asked I laughingly said American coffee. She turned up several days later with two tins. The next time I tried something harder, as a test you understand. I asked her for typewriter ribbons. She returned with four, of West German manufacture. At various times she brought me carbon paper, copies of an American magazine called News-something-or-other, some Swiss homeopathic sleeping pills, an English knife sharpener and some French headache suppositories. Ha! Suppositories for a headache! Only the French would think of that!"

"What about Nadezhda?" insists Pravdin.

"Nadezhda moved in about three months after me," Zoya continues. "Her story was much the same as mine. Her building was being razed to make way for a new hospital. Which hasn't been built yet. But that's another story. She searched for an apartment for weeks, but everything she heard about seemed to disappear before she got there. Someone whispered something about a Druse, she went to him and wound up here. It took several weeks of talking about various things until we stumbled on what we had in common: my husband defending her grandfather. Nadezhda said it was a coincidence that had brought us together, but I always thought it was fate."

"You were both wrong," comments Pravdin. "It was the Druse."

Zoya nods. "It was Chuvash Al-hakim bi'amrillahi," she agrees. "I must say you were less obvious; I couldn't understand what you had to do with us until the manuscripts arrived. Then I saw the lovely logic of it. The Druse has organized the perfect team: the granddaughter of the real author, the wife of the only member of the 1929 commission to support that authorship and a hustler who is neither mute nor crazy, who can figure out how to right this wrong. Armed with the manuscripts—"

"The manuscripts," Pravdin cries, "are a mystery." He is intoxicated with panic. "Where did he get them? And why does he want to ruin Frolov?"

"What does it matter?" declares Zoya. "His motive may be personal. Or political. Maybe someone in the superstructure is out to sink Frolov and is using the Druse. Who cares about the why? What matters is that we have the proof—the original manuscripts of *The Deep Don* in Krukov's handwriting."

Pravdin, calmer, only shakes his head. "There is still something in all this business I can't put my thumb on."

CHAPTER 5

Mother Russia
is certified . . .

Mother Russia is certified, Pravdin berates himself under his breath, but I'm the one who is off his rocker.

The man at the next urinal, a trim captain in the regular Army, hears Pravdin rambling on. "Were you addressing me, comrade citizen?"

Instinctively Pravdin casts a quick glance at his neighbor's penis, notes that he's not circumcised. "Not at all, honored captain," he replies hurriedly, hunching forward into the urinal to hide his own covenant with a God in whom he doesn't believe. "I was mulling over some lines from one of Lenin's articles. You know the one; it's called, 'What is to be done?'"

Staring suspiciously, the militia captain zips up, wipes his palms on his trousers as he leaves. Clutching his briefcase tightly under his arm, Pravdin shakes out a few last drops, retracts, bends his knees, pulls up his zipper and straightens at the same time, scrawls with his felt-tip pen above the urinal:

The shortage shall be divided among the peasants (Anon: Pravdin considers himself something of an armchair agronomist). *That's it,* Pravdin thinks, *no more procrastinating,* and he dashes into the corridor in search of the room marked "Public Prosecutor."

He has changed his mind a dozen times a day for the last week. Even after he photocopied portions of the manuscripts at the Lenin Library (a "favor" that cost him a German edition in braille of *The Story of O* and a two-year-old Sony four-band portable) and hid the original, he wasn't sure he would go through with it. "Maybe yes, maybe no," was the best Mother Russia could get out of him when she pushed him into a moral corner.

"Maybe yes, maybe no," she scolded, wagging her fly swatter under his nose. "Your life is one big maybe yes, maybe no. For God's sake, take a stand. Run a risk. Walk on water. Move mountains. Change the world. Work up a sweat from a noneconomic activity! A little idealism is good for the digestion, heartburn, headaches, neuritis, neuralgia and sexual potency."

"Idealism is an ideal," Pravdin protested gloomily, "not a formula for everyday survival."

"Ha! Survival!" cried Zoya, seizing upon the word as if it were an admission of guilt that slipped accidentally from the lips of the accused. "All you think about is survival."

"Survival, little mother, is a habit I don't want to kick."

"Will you or won't you?" she demanded, exasperated to the point where she had trouble breathing.

"Maybe yes, maybe no."

Nadezhda took another tack. "If you think it is too dangerous," she wrote once, "perhaps you shouldn't."

"Nobody will criticize you if you back out now," she wrote on another occasion.

"Go ahead with it only if you feel it is the right thing to do," she wrote the following day, slipped the folded note into his shirt pocket, stood on tiptoes and kissed him squarely on his bloodless lips.

"You win," Pravdin told Zoya over camomile tea the next morning. He rolled his bloodshot eyes in mock horror. "Let's see who will surrender to unarmed truth."

The waiting room outside the public prosecutor's office is as hushed as a library reading room. "Take a number," the clerk at the door whispers to Pravdin.

"I've got it," he says, thinking she is about to try and read his mind.

"From the box," she hisses when she sees what he's up to.

"Oh," Pravdin says out loud. A half dozen heads swivel toward the sound of his voice; he expects to be shushed. He takes a cardboard number, moves to a place on the wooden bench next to a stony-faced war veteran whose one remaining eye is fixed on the shadowy crotch of a young girl across the room. Pravdin follows his gaze, sees she is wearing the shortest miniskirt he has ever seen.

After a while the one-eyed war veteran pokes Pravdin with his elbow. "If miniskirts go up another centimeter," he snorts, "there's going to be a revolution."

"We've already used up our quota of revolutions, friend," Pravdin replies sourly.

The one-eyed war veteran leans toward Pravdin, talks to him while continuing to stare at the girl. "What are you here for?" he asks conversationally.

"I'm here to complain about doctors," Pravdin tells him.

"It's this way: I share my one-room flat with my mother, who is a hundred and twenty-two years old. Touch wood." (His knuckles rap on the bench.) "The problem is that we're a little cramped for space and she looks as if she's going to live forever."

"But what's that got to do with doctors?"

"What's that got to do with doctors," Pravdin explains, his voice rising in desperation, "is that they've ruined pneumonia!"

The one-eyed war veteran turns toward Pravdin for the first time and regards him through his narrowed eye. "You're crazy, you know," he says seriously.

Pravdin's palm slaps his high forehead. "Crazy is what I am!"

A middle-aged woman with a small boy in tow emerges from the inner sanctum. "Number one forty-one," the clerk calls. The one-eyed war veteran glances at his number, grunts, heaves himself off the bench and starts toward the door of the prosecutor's office. Pravdin averts his eyes from the miniskirted siren, loses himself in thought. He remembers sitting for fourteen hours on exactly the same kind of wooden bench, clutching his throbbing thumb broken under the heel of a KGB interrogator, waiting to see the officer with the blue shoulder boards. The interview, when it finally came, lasted two minutes. The officer, a young man with a permanent pout, leafed through the dossier marked "Pravdin, R. I.," ranted about some conspiracy or other, ordered Pravdin to name names, asked Pravdin in the name of Stalin to name names, begged Pravdin for his own good to name names, shrugged, uncapped his fountain pen, wrote something, signed it with a flourish, looked up and said, "Eight years." In his mind's eye Pravdin sees himself standing before the officer, only vaguely comprehending what has happened to him, mumbling his thanks (*his thanks!* Even now Pravdin cringes with humiliation when he remembers he *thanked* the bastard), executing a military about-face and marching briskly off as if his cadenced step would testify to his loyalty to Mother Russia and Papa Stalin.

"Number one forty-two."

Frightened by the pounding of his heart, Pravdin looks up at the clerk.

"Number one forty-two," the clerk repeats. Across the room the girl in the miniskirt uncrosses and recrosses her legs, stares inquisitively at Pravdin. "Are you or aren't you?" the expression on her face seems to ask.

"Maybe yes, maybe no," Pravdin mutters.

"I beg your pardon?" the clerk says.

Pravdin rises on weak legs, still not sure he'll go through with it. Droplets of sweat break out like pimples on his forehead. He tries to tally up the pros and cons but can only think of the cons. And Mother Russia telling him to walk on water. And Nadezhda's cool kiss on his bloodless lips. And in he goes.

The first things he notices are the public prosecutor's fingernails (thick, cut squarely, a sure sign of rural roots) and a small hand-lettered plaque on the wall under the obligatory photograph of Lenin that reads, "Civic courage is rarer than military valor."

"You really believe that?" Pravdin asks, indicating with his nose the plaque under Comrade Lenin haranguing workers at the Finland Station.

The prosecutor, an intense young man with thick wavy hair and a broad open face, nods solemnly. "With all respect to your medals," he says, "I do. Military valor requires you to do what, in doing, wins approval. Civic courage requires you to go against the grain; to do things that people disapprove of. Civic courage requires moral judgments."

The prosecutor speaks with quiet conviction and Pravdin

realizes he has landed before a rare bird—and from the look of him, one fresh from the sticks. His suit is the tip-off: a shiny navy worsted, it is much too thick for this time of year and indicates that the prosecutor hasn't been in Moscow long enough to pick up one of the lightweight models available in the special stores set aside for bosses.

"Let me begin by offering you my personal congratulations," Pravdin ventures.

The young prosecutor is startled. "Why?"

"The promotion is why," Pravdin explains. "Not to mention the transfer. Before Moscow where were you posted?"

"I was in Alma Ata," the prosecutor acknowledges. His face has reddened. "But how do you know these things?"

"I have friends in high places." Pravdin winks. "I could use influence, but I don't take advantage of my name. I wait my turn like any ordinary citizen. When my number is called I present my body, scarred in defense of the Motherland, exactly as if I were a nobody."

"It is only fair to tell you," the prosecutor informs Pravdin gravely, "that I am not impressed with physical scars."

"Mental scars then," Pravdin clutches at a straw. He lowers his voice, gestures to the walls to indicate they have ears. "When I was thirteen I was picked up for writing antifascist slogans on the Kremlin walls. I chose the wrong moment; Papa Stalin had just signed on the dotted line alongside von Ribbentrop. I was accused of premature antifascism and packed off to a Komsomol camp, where the big problem was premature ejaculation. Mental scars, friend, are what I have more than my share of."

"Am I to assume that you are a member of the Party?" the Prosecutor inquires.

"I'm better," Pravdin assures him earnestly. "I *believe* in communism. For me the second holy of holies is the British

Museum Reading Room, the birthplace of pure Marxism, the only twentieth century ism to convey a sense of morality without religion." The prosecutor purses his lips; Pravdin, trying to decipher the signals, wonders if he has stepped on toes. "Not that I have anything against religion," he quickly adds, imagining the prosecutor's old babushkaed mother trudging through ankle-deep mud toward some dilapidated church.

The prosecutor, intrigued, leans forward, elbows on the desk, fingers laced under his chin; it is the gesture of someone twice his age and it makes him look, to Pravdin's eye, somehow biblical. "You believe in original sin then?" he asks politely.

Floundering, not sure what high ground to claim as his own, Pravdin tries to sidestep. "I believe in original naiveté," he quips.

"But original naiveté is the original sin," the prosecutor warns.

"Not at all," Pravdin hears himself say. "Naiveté is no sin. It is a blessing in disguise, a state of grace, a chain-mail Eisenhower jacket."

The prosecutor frowns. "What is it you have come to tell me? Against whom do you wish to lodge a complaint?"

Pravdin takes a deep breath, holds it until his eyes bulge. "It's this way," he begins, expelling a lungful of air. And he tells the prosecutor about the handwritten manuscripts that prove that Krukov, not Frolov, is the real author of *The Deep Don*.

The prosecutor listens intently to the story, asks Pravdin to repeat it a second time while he takes notes. When Pravdin has gone through it all again the prosecutor asks to see the manuscripts. Pravdin laughs nervously. "The manuscripts are what I don't have," he explains. "They have been stashed in a safe place. A kind of insurance policy is what it is, if you get my drift. But I have the next best thing." And he dips into his leather briefcase and pulls out a sheaf of photocopies of manuscript pages. "Listen," Pravdin says excitedly —he pushes two sheets across the desk under the prosecutor's nose—"you remember the part in *The Deep Don* where the Cossacks find worms in their meat, draw their sabres, arrest the worms, march them up to the company commander and announce they've brought in some prisoners. Look, here the story is recounted in a letter written by Krukov to his father-in-law in 1919. And here is the same story, again in Krukov's hand, in a manuscript page of his novel. And then it turns up several years later in Frolov's book!"

The prosecutor reads, rereads the photocopies of the letter and the manuscript page, studying each line through a magnifying glass. "It goes without saying the handwriting will have to be authenticated," he says carefully.

"Without saying is how it goes," Pravdin agrees eagerly.

"If it turns out that this documentation is authentic," the prosecutor continues—Pravdin catches the treble-shift of excitement in his voice—"we will have a very important case on our hands."

"Handled discreetly," Pravdin exclaims gleefully, "it could revolutionize Russia."

The prosecutor rises, Pravdin follows suit. "Speak to no one about this," he instructs Pravdin formally.

"No one is whom I'll speak to," he vows.

"Be back here tomorrow at nine."

"Back here is where I'll be."

The prosecutor reaches across the desk and offers Pravdin his hand. "Russia is a country of rusty-hinged shutters waiting to be oiled and opened," he says gravely. "Together we will open one and let in some air."

"Only pay attention," Pravdin cautions the public prosecutor, "not to catch cold from the draft."

Suppressing the urge to whistle, Pravdin heads across town for a rendezvous with the All-Union Institute for Household Technology. On Gorky Street he glances at his two wristwatches (Moscow time, Greenwich Mean Time), looks up to compare them to the giant digital clock on the side of the post office, which keeps flashing 9:32:32 like a needle stuck in a groove.

"You wouldn't happen to have the correct hour?" inquires a well-dressed woman in her seventies. She is holding the hand of a fifty-year-old man who heels at her side like a dog. His coat is neatly buttoned to the neck, his collar turned down.

"Ice cream, mama," the fifty-year-old man whines, tugging at his mother's hand.

"Dear Madam, it is twenty minutes past seven in Greenwich, England, and twelve minutes past eleven here in Moscow," Pravdin informs her.

"But how is that possible?" the woman demands.

"What I see is what I know," Pravdin snaps, hurtles, head angled like a bull's, on down Gorky. At the All-Union Institute for Household Technology, a heavy-set woman sips mint-flavored milk and listens, her features sagging in apathy, to the Q-Tip spiel.

"The Q-Tip is an idea whose time has come," Pravdin argues passionately. "Before you can build communism you must construct socialism. Before socialism, an advanced industrial society. And whoever heard of an advanced industrial society without Q-Tips!"

The woman fingers the Q-Tip as if it has sexual possibilities, shakes her head regretfully, says nothing can be done without careful examination of the medical implications by the Department of Medicine at Moscow University.

So that the morning isn't a total loss Pravdin delivers a diamond-tipped Shure cartridge and two Beatle records to a disc jockey at the radio station, a set of *National Geographics* to the wife of a member of the Supreme Soviet, a year's supply of West German birth control pills to a famous folk singer, then takes the Metro back to the Kremlin and walks over to the Hotel Moskva where he presents himself at a luncheon honoring the author of a new book that explores the possibilities of time travel.

"Pravdin, R. I.," he announces to the near-sighted spinster editor fanning herself with the guest list, "at your beck and call." Leaning closer he tells her:

"Absolutely no autographs—except for you, elegant lady." He uncaps his felt-tipped pen and scrawls across her guest list, "To my dear friend—" He looks up questioningly.

"Natalia," the spinster replies. "Natalia Mikhaylova."

"—Natalia Mikhaylova, the mere glimpse of whose lascivious eyes and luscious body have permanently wrecked my hormonal balance." With a flourish he signs, "Robespierre Isayevich Pravdin."

Flashing his crooked smile, Pravdin bows from the waist and brushes past the stunned woman into the luncheon hall.

Friedemann T. stands with his back to a mural depicting prosperous peasants during a bountiful harvest, a glass of slivovitz in one hand, a wedge of cold quiche in the other, nodding noncommittally to a bald man with bad breath. The bald man retreats as Pravdin approaches.

"What are we here?" Friedemann T. whispers desperately.

"What we are here is time travel," Pravdin informs him.

Friedemann T.'s features relax. "Time travel." He ponders this for a moment. "That's a new one." He rocks on the balls of his feet, shrugs his cape back onto his shoulders, raises his voice. "Frankly, I'm skeptical. If time travel is possible, why haven't we been visited by people from the future?"

Pravdin deftly snags a sandwich from a passing tray. "Maybe there is no future," he ventures. "Maybe we are the point of time."

"Statistically unlikely," Friedemann T. dismisses the suggestion.

"Someone has to be the point of time," Pravdin insists.

"Even that's not clear," says Friedemann T. "The trouble with you is you're a prisoner of logic. Why should every event have a cause, and why should every cause precede its effect? How do we know that the atom doesn't consist of the radiations that it gives off? Where is it ordained that a window can't break before the ball is thrown at it?"

Pravdin thinks about this for a moment. "What tortures me," he says—he waves across the room to nobody in particular—"is: if I travel back in time I may disrupt events so that they create a future that doesn't contain me, so I don't exist to travel back in time."

Friedemann T. laughs at a thought.

"What's funny?" Pravdin demands.

"Maybe," Friedemann T. says—he gestures toward the crowd milling around the author and laughs again—"maybe we've already traveled back in time."

Later, as they start toward the exit, Friedemann T. steers Pravdin into the men's room. "You should have told me, you know," he chastises him. "I'm supposed to be a friend."

"Told you what?" Pravdin wants to know, his voice slipping over the edge into nervousness.

"If I knew about what, I wouldn't be asking you to tell me," says Friedemann T. "I hope you know what you're doing," he adds in a low voice.

"What for God's sake am I doing?" demands Pravdin.

"That was precisely what the militia major wanted to know." Friedemann T. turns to go, adds with icy politeness:

"Do me the service of waiting a minute or two so we won't be seen leaving together."

"What leaving together?" Pravdin cries hysterically. "About what are you talking?"

But Friedemann T. has already slipped out of the men's room.

In the street Pravdin glances over his shoulder every few seconds, doesn't notice anybody following him, stops to scrawl on the rear wall of the Union of Journalists:

Publish *and* perish

(Anon: Pravdin has recently skimmed some Abram Tertz stories in *samizdat*), hurries on to the synagogue for his appointment with the beardless assistant rabbi.

"The answer is *nyet*," the rabbi cries when he catches sight of Pravdin.

"How can you give an answer when you don't know the question?" argues Pravdin. The rabbi scurries down the aisle past the neon Star of David into the bare vestibule that serves as an office. Pravdin is hard on his heels.

"It doesn't matter the question, the answer is no," the rabbi repeats, unwinding the frayed tefillen from his forearm.

"That's not biblical," protests Pravdin.

The rabbi turns on him angrily. "We don't live in biblical times," he wails. "We are no longer the chosen people. You are not some big shot Old Testament prophet come to lead us in your Eisenhower jacket and basketball sneakers to the promised land. If the Red Sea parts tomorrow it will be to let some capitalist Cain under contract to some Arab Abel drill for oil."

"For God's sake calm yourself, rabbi," Pravdin urges.

"It's not as if I yelled the secret name of God outside the holy of holies."

The assistant rabbi settles into a chair, closes his eyes, sucks in air through hairy nostrils. "Be my guest, pose the question," he says hoarsely.

Pravdin leans across the table until he is breathing into the rabbi's face. "Instant matzos," he begins, "is an idea whose time has come. Thesis: powdered matzos direct from Tel Aviv. Antithesis: holy water from the River Jordan. Synthesis:"—Pravdin sways back, pauses for theatrical effect—"all the matzos your heart desires for the High Holy Days."

"I've heard the question, you're my witness," the assistant rabbi says with controlled calm, "and the answer is still no." He springs from his chair, takes Pravdin firmly under the elbow, steers him toward the door. "What are you up to these days that they come here asking about you?" he whispers. Pravdin starts to reply but the assistant rabbi holds up a palm. "Better you don't tell me. What you don't tell me I don't know. If I don't know it can't be a conspiracy. Listen, Robespierre Isayevich, you want to do something for the Jews, go become a Christian."

Pravdin, wounded, clings to the doorknob like a child on his first day at school. "It's too late to convert," he whines. "I'm circumcised."

The assistant rabbi, surprisingly strong, pries his fingers off the knob one by one. "Circumcise your heart," he advises, and he shoves him out the door.

Mother Russia pulls her fox furs tightly around her neck, leans over the stove to taste a spoonful of soybean soup, swallows, grimaces, adds a pinch of salt.

Pravdin, moody, mumbles unintelligibly.

"What did you say?" Zoya takes the seat across the table from Pravdin.

"Nothing is what I said," he answers sullenly.

She pats his arm reassuringly. "What nothing?" she coaxes. "Out with it, give?"

From behind the closed door of Mother Russia's room comes the muted cry of Kerensky:

"*Waak, waak, power to the powerful.*"

"Make an effort," urges Zoya.

"I walk on water," Pravdin finally blurts out, "and soybean soup is all you think about."

"Oh Robespierre, you don't understand. I'm superstitious is all. I'm afraid it will go away if we talk about it." Zoya covers her mouth with her hand, talks through her fingers. "His nails sound respectable. Do you really think your prosecutor is a serious personage?"

"He is young and wet behind the ears," Pravdin says quietly, "but he's honest, if that's possible anymore."

"I came across an honest bureaucrat once," recalls Zoya. "It was in thirty-seven or thirty-eight. I was trying to post a package to my husband. The official advised me not to bother because the camp guards took everything for themselves."

"Zoya Aleksandrovna, sometimes I think nostalgia is your strongest emotion," Pravdin says.

Mother Russia's eyes lose their focus. "Yes, it's true what you say. For me the past is more"—she searches for the right word—"intense than the present."

"The murder of your husband—"

"Oh, I don't mean only the arrests and the camps and the war. I mean the *past*. I remember when I was a little girl and my father took the family to the countryside to pick mushrooms. It was a great occasion because it was my first ride in an automobile. My father had had one for several months but he had considered it too dangerous for the women in the family. One day, only God knows why, he relented. We drove with planks strapped to the side of the car.

It was just after the last snows had melted and the roads were full of potholes. At each hole my father stopped and we children would lay down the planks and he would drive across as if he were traversing some deep, dangerous gorge. Then we would pick up the planks and strap them back onto the side of the car. It seems to me, now that I think of it, that the mushrooms we picked had more taste than the ones I find nowadays. But that's another story." Zoya absently pets the head of one of her foxes. "You were naughty not to invite me to lunch," she scolds Pravdin. "I'm very interested in extraterrestrial phenomena and time travel and that kind of thing."

"You don't really believe in all that nonsense?"

"I most certainly do," Zoya replies indignantly. "What was the pillar of cloud by day and the pillar of fire by night that led the Israelites out of Egypt if not some kind of rocket? What about the Tibetan books that describe prehistoric machines as pearls in the sky? What about the Samerangana Sutrodhara, which has chapter and verse describing spaceships whose tails spout fire and quicksilver? What about the Mahabharata, which talks about machines that could fly forward or upward or downward? Ha! What about that?"

"What about, what about," Pravdin mimics. "What about the prosecutor making another appointment to see me?"

"Shhhhhhh," Zoya whispers. She lays her bony forefinger against her lips. "You'll put a hex on it."

"Help, help, waak, waak," cries Vladimir Ilyich from the other room.

Mother Russia and Pravdin attack the soybean soup; Pravdin meets his spoon halfway, blows noisily, swallows. After dinner Zoya abruptly excuses herself to put the finishing touches on another zinger to Singer.

"She's the only person I know who's obsessed with a

sewing machine," Pravdin tells Nadezhda when she arrives with a satchel full of tins of Norwegian sardines.

"Every healthy person needs an obsession," Nadezhda writes. "Zoya's body is too old for sex."

"Nobody's body is too old for sex," Pravdin fires back. No sooner have the words passed his lips than blood rushes to his face.

Nadezhda turns to stare at him, her head cocked co-quettishly, "*Tiens*," she writes, "there are parts of you we haven't been to yet."

"The same needs everyone has are what I have," Pravdin gives ground grudgingly.

Nadezhda scribbles furiously, taunts him with a slip of paper on which she has written:

"Power, prestige, money, money, money."

Pravdin stubbornly defends himself. "What you don't know, it's easy to make fun of."

"What makes Pravdin run?" writes Nadezhda.

"It seems to me," Pravdin answers, his face twisting into a crooked smile, his voice thick with self-mockery, "that my whole life I've wanted to do an exploit. Like those knights in shining armor with long lances riding animals they could identify."

"That's for the ego," Nadezhda writes. "What's for the body?"

Pravdin reads the note, crumples it, flings it across the table at Nadezhda. "Sex is what's for the body!" he cries.

Nadezhda regards him for a long moment, comes to a decision, leads him by the hand into her room, locks the door behind her, pulls back the cover from the bed, kicks off her sandals, turns on the radio, begins to remove her clothes.

"Sex is an idea whose time has come," Pravdin explodes jubilantly, flinging away his Eisenhower jacket. "Thesis: the male organ, erect. Antithesis: the female organ, moist. Synthesis:"—he shouts it out in a voice raw with lust—"sexual intercourse!"

They make love, guided by instinct more than ardor, in the light of the small bulb that illuminates the radio dial. The springs of the bed and the floorboards squeak beneath them. Their bodies become slick with sweat; there is a sucking sound when their chests press together. Pravdin kisses her with lips that have lost their erogenousness from disuse, feels her wet palms on his bony flanks pulling him inside her and off he comes—too soon, too soon!

"Too soon, sorry," he mutters as he collapses on her, dizzy with effort and gasping for air. Nadezhda twines her arms and legs around him and holds him close.

After a while she shifts uncomfortably under his weight. He rolls off her and they lie side by side staring at the ceiling until they are dry. Then Nadezhda props herself up on an elbow, makes him hard, climbs on top and they make love again, this time slowly, meticulously, as if tuning an instrument. The squeaking of the bed springs and the floorboards is more rhythmic. The second coming, a triumph of technique, is at hand. Pravdin utters a long low moan of pleasure and sinks back onto the mattress; the squeaking continues for a few seconds, Nadezhda arches her back and then silently folds herself into the angles of his body.

Somewhere in the building a toilet flushes; water rushes through pipes in the walls. Nadezhda leaps lightly from the bed, rummages in a dresser, returns with a towel, wipes Pravdin and then the sheet. She settles cross-legged on the bed, her back against the wall, writes something and passes him the note. He leans closer to the radio to read it in the light from the dial. She has written: "Love making makes time stand still for me."

Pravdin borrows her pad, scribbles, "Pleasure is a clock like any other," tears off the page, passes it to her.

While she is reading that he hands her another page that says, "Imaginary conversations are what I have with you all day long."

"What do I say?" she writes.

"I tell you," Pravdin writes, "there are between us simple things that have the possibility of becoming complex. You think a moment, reply, 'Yes, there are things between us, but they are complex and have the possibility of becoming simple.' "

"I look young but I talk old," Nadezhda writes. "What else?"

"I tell you," Pravdin writes, "there are between us simdevelop. You think a moment, reply, "Emotion is what we must develop. Philosophy attacks like erosion, emotion like a chisel.' "

"I tell you," Pravdin writes, "emotion is what I'm not comfortable with. You think a moment, reply, 'Your problem is you try to pry apart an emotion with words when you should be riding it the way a surfer skims along on a wave.' "

"I tell you," Pravdin writes, "people are hooked on words. You think a moment, reply, 'People exist, like minnows between rocks, swimming in the spaces between the words.' "

Pravdin reaches out with his primitively long, broken, badly set thumb and presses Nadezhda's nipple as if it is a doorbell. With the other hand he passes her a page on which he has written:

Yes ☐		Now ☐	
No ☐		Later ☐	
Maybe ☐		Tomorrow ☐	
Above ☐		Conventional ☐	
Below ☐		Unconventional ☐	

Nadezhda playfully fills in the squares, returns the paper with X's next to "Yes," "Now," "Above," "Unconventional."

Pravdin laughs wickedly, lunges for Nadezhda, who makes no effort to escape.

Pravdin, descending noisily from the attic as if he has been there all night, yawns casually, but Nadezhda gives the game away when she turns up for breakfast with a streak of blue dye between her burning eyes—concocted from the juice of an herb called usma that she once bought from an old Uzbek at the open market.

"So that's how it is," Mother Russia exclaims when she sees the streak, and she ceremonially embraces Nadezhda and then Pravdin, kissing them each on the left shoulder and the forehead in the Uzbek manner of greating young lovers.

Count your blessings, Pravdin tells himself as he starts down the wooden staircase. *You're reasonably healthy, you can still get it up three times in one night and you live in the last wooden house in central Moscow. Touch wood.* (His bony knuckles rap on the polished banister.)

At the screen door Porfiry Yakolev, the weatherman, and Master Embalmer Makusky smirk when they catch sight of Pravdin and hurry down the alley whispering excitedly. General Shuvkin emerges into the sunlight, sees Pravdin, winks, pats him on the back with his good arm. "Over and above the call of duty," he snaps, starts off after Yakolev and Makusky.

"So you made it with Nadezhda," comments Ophelia Long Legs, sitting on the front steps embroidering the bell-bottoms of a pair of jeans. "It's the floorboards," she explains when she sees Pravdin's puzzled expression. "Cheer up," she adds, "at your age three times in one night is nothing to be ashamed of."

* * *

Pravdin, scurrying along behind the Church of All Mourn-
ers across the river from the Kremlin, stops to tighten a
sneaker lace, glances apprehensively at the clear heavens, skywrites with the tip of his deformed thumb:

Jesus, sauve Toi

(Anon: Pravdin has always been free with his ecumenical
counsel), races off for his appointment with the prosecutor.

At the Ministry, Pravdin snatches his cardboard number
and takes his place on the bench between a starchy Muscovite
with bifocals peering at the long gray columns of *Pravda*
and a blond Georgian boy carrying a stringless guitar. "What
are you here for?" the Georgian asks conversationally.

"I'm here to complain about Honored Artist of the
Soviet Union Frolov," Pravdin explains. "It's this way: During
the Civil War he swiped the manuscripts for *The Deep Don*
from a White Russian officer named Krukov and published
it under his own name."

The Georgian shrinks away from Pravdin to avoid con-
tamination. "You're off your rocker, you know," he says
seriously.

Pravdin's palm slaps his high forehead. "Off my rocker is
what I am!"

When his number is called Pravdin hurtles headlong into
the prosecutor's office. "Robespierre Isayevich Pravdin at your
—your—at your . . ." Pravdin's bloodless lips continue to
move, words form but no sound emerges; he is speechless
with astonishment. He stares wide eyed at the man behind
the desk, then at the photograph of Lenin haranguing workers at the Finland Station. "Where's 'Civic courage is
rare' and so forth and so on? Where is the public prosecutor?"

"You are looking at the public prosecutor," the prosecutor says coldly.

"The prosecutor I spoke with in this office yesterday is who I'm not looking at," insists Pravdin. "Even your fingernails are different."

"You're off your rocker," the prosecutor, a sallow-skinned functionary, tells Pravdin. "I've been in this office every workday for fourteen years except for authorized vacations and the time I fractured my tibia skiing in Zakopane."

Pravdin tries to flash his crooked smile, manages only a grimace. Backpedaling toward the half open door, he does a little jig and mumbles in a singsong voice:

"Unarmed truth is not an idea whose time has come."

CHAPTER 6

Pravdin, buried in *Pravda*'s
back pages . . .

Pravdin, buried in *Pravda*'s back pages, glances up, sees that
the train is just pulling out of the Kiyevskaya station, goes
back to his newspaper hunting for the innocuous items that
contain the real news. He reads about the charges brought
against two brothers in Minsk with obviously Jewish names; it
seems they had set up a nailpolish remover factory in their
basement, pasted "Made in Amerika" labels on the product
and sold it for exorbitant prices on the black market. (They
were tripped up when an alert client's suspicions were aroused
by the *k* in "Amerika.") He reads about a candidate member
of the Politburo with an obviously Armenian name who has
been farmed out to run a tractor factory in Kirgizia; the offi-

cial explanation is "mental fatigue," but Pravdin has heard on the grapevine that the man in question had been discovered *in flagrante delicto* with the wife of one of the upwardly mobile directors of the Komsomol. Pravdin's eye catches a tiny item sandwiched between the soccer scores and an account of an extraordinary rainfall in Mongolia: the Kremlin chimes that regularly sound the hour have not been heard for two days; the official explanation is "metal fatigue," but Pravdin has heard on the grapevine that Brezhnev suffers from migraines and has been complaining about the noise.

The train pulls into a station, Pravdin catches sight of a sign that says "Studencheskaya" and dashes from the car just as the doors start to close. At the far end of the car a heavy-set man in a blue raincoat and a flat short-brimmed fedora struggles with the door to keep it from closing, overpowers it, squeezes through onto the platform. Pravdin sprints up the stairs to the street level, darts behind a kiosk selling lottery tickets, waits. The man in the blue raincoat comes panting up the stairs, stops short, looks around.

Pravdin walks directly up to him. "Professional is what you're not," he whispers nervously to the man in the blue raincoat. "I know you're following me."

"If you know I'm following you," the man informs him, "you're meant to know I'm following you."

"That I hadn't thought of," Pravdin admits. He turns, wanders uncertainly for a few blocks, then briskly cuts across Kutuzovsky Prospect and ducks into the cemetery, with the man in the blue raincoat not far behind. In the cemetery Pravdin joins a funeral procession for a few steps, then races down a pathway, stops to catch his breath crouching behind a headstone, on the back of which he scrawls in chalk:

So here it is at last, the Distinguished Thing

(H. James: Pravdin is queer for dying words). After a while

he makes a run for a side gate and loses himself among the pedestrians in the street.

At Poklonnaya, he spots a postal box, takes from his briefcase a batch of zingers Mother Russia has given him to mail, notes their addressees (Mr. Singer of the Singer Sewing Machine Company, Comrade Chairman Leonid Brezhnev of the Politburo, Premier Pompidou of the Elysée Palace and one to the "Person in charge of cholesterol" at the World Health Organization in Geneva), slips them through the slit. Two blocks further along he enters an apartment house, lingers on the third floor landing long enough to make sure he isn't being followed, then climbs to the sixth floor, crosses over to another wing, descends to the fourth floor and presses with his deformed thumb on a bell. Friedemann T. opens the door a crack, sees Pravdin's face peering at him, tries to slam it shut again. Pravdin's sneaker, strategically wedged, prevents him.

"For God's sake," Pravdin wails, "my toes!"

"You can alleviate the pain," Friedemann T. explains calmly, "by the simple expedient of removing your preposterous shoe from my communal doorstep."

"I'm here to offer you a hundred rubles for half an hour of your precious time," Pravdin cries.

The pressure on Pravdin's sneaker eases. "A hundred rubles, you say?" Friedemann T. pokes his head into the corridor, looks both ways, motions Pravdin into the apartment with his hand. He locks the door behind him, leads the way into his bedroom, locks that door too, turns on the radio. "Were you followed here?" he demands.

"Touch wood, that's all finished with," says Pravdin. "A simple case of misunderstanding on the part of one of my important clients."

"What do I have to do for the hundred?" Friedemann T. wants to know.

"It's this way," Pravdin explains. "I have a client who happens to be an American journalist. He's willing to pay two hundred rubles for an interview with a Bolshoi choreographer who was fired because he applied for an exit visa to Israel. I figure you could pull it off easily, and we'll split the two hundred down the middle. What do you say?"

Friedemann T. raises a forefinger to his pursed lips, rocks thoughtfully on the soles of his feet. "Dear boy," he muses, "I only applied for my exit visa when the police confiscated my choreographic notations for a new ballet based on Solzhenitsyn's *The First Circle*."

"I've always felt," Pravdin speaks up on cue, "that the performing arts were obliged to pick up where the creative arts left off."

"I have it on good authority," Friedemann T. goes on, "that the decision to suppress my ballet was taken on the Politburo level. I can tell you"—the painter lowers his voice—"that a candidate member of the Politburo with an obviously Armenian name was packed off to Kirgizia for favoring the production. But I refuse to be intimidated."

"I've always maintained," Pravdin is well into the game now, "that the bosses have two choices: they can convince us or they can kill us. Ha! That's a good line. I'll bet you wish you'd said that."

"When your journalist friend shows up," Friedemann T. comments, "I will."

"For you, good news," Pravdin tells Hull, the American journalist. They are sharing a shelf at a stand-up coffee bar on the top floor of GUM. "The Bolshoi choreographer you asked about is whom I found. Two hundred rubles is what it will cost you—half for me, half for him."

"Two hundred is kind of steep," Hull complains.

"Work is what he's out of," Pravdin explains. "He needs the money to leave the country."

"And you?" Hull asks. "What do you need the hundred for?"

"To stay in the country is what I need it for." He passes Hull a folded slip of paper with Friedemann T.'s name and address on it. Hull pockets the paper, hands Pravdin a wad of ten-ruble notes. There is an excited rush of shoppers in the passageway outside the coffee bar. A woman with dyed red hair pokes her head in, calls to a friend, "Tania, come quickly, they've got a shipment of West German electric hair curlers," disappears. All the women in the bar, and some of the men, abandon their coffee in mid-sip and dash after the woman with the dyed red hair.

"You don't need electric hair curlers?" asks Hull, his voice thick with sarcasm.

"I saw the salesgirl on my way in," replies Pravdin. "She put two sets aside for me."

Hull shakes his head in admiration. "You're one in a million, Pravdin."

"The sense of that is what I don't get," says Pravdin. "What means this 'One in a million'?"

"It means you stand out in a crowd."

"That," Pravdin agrees, "has always been my problem."

Pravdin starts to leave but Hull puts a hand on his arm. "You've seen the item in the *Chronicle of Current Events?*" he asks casually.

Pravdin looks at him suspiciously. "Clandestine anti-Soviet publications are what I don't subscribe to," he says. "What item?"

"They claim that someone in Moscow has come up with original manuscripts proving that Frolov is not the real author of *The Deep Don.*"

"What's that got to do with me?" Pravdin demands hysterically.

Hull studies Pravdin, his eyes more feverish than ever. "Listen, I'd be willing to put a good deal of money on the line for an introduction to the someone in question and a peek at the manuscripts. Hey, Pravdin, where's the fire?"

But Pravdin, abandoning the idea of collecting his hair curlers, is removing his panic-stricken heart from GUM.

On Gorky Street, Pravdin looks at his watch with the water vapor under the crystal, sees that it is almost eleven, Moscow time, stops at a public phone to call the Danish diplomat who has agreed to trade his entire pop record collection for an icon.

"Knud Thestrop is whom I want to speak to," Pravdin says when the phone is picked up at the other end.

"Knud Thestrop has left the country," a man's voice says.

"What left the country?" cries Pravdin. "I recognize your voice. How is it you can say you left the country when you're standing there talking to me? What about our deal?"

"I'm sorry," the man's voice says nervously. "You'll have to understand. Thestrop is no longer in the country." The phone clicks dead.

Pravdin inserts another two-kopeck coin, dials the private number of the post office official responsible for confiscating (and supposedly burning) foreign-language books that are sent by mail to the country. Every two weeks or so Pravdin stops by, picks up a package of books for resale on the black market, splits the proceeds with the official.

The phone rings four times, then a recorded female voice comes on. She says:

"I'm sorry, but the number you reached doesn't exist. Please consult the phone book in the central post office. I'm sorry, but the number you reached doesn't exist. Please consult—"

Pravdin, furious, frightened, drops the receiver back on the hook, hurries over to Aragvi for a luncheon in honor of a French doctor who is a world-renowned specialist on the inner ear.

"Pravdin, R. I.," Pravdin announces to the pretty young woman with the guest list. "Doctor of micro-philately."

The woman takes in the unkempt reddish hair going off in all directions at once, the Eisenhower jacket with the four medals dangling on the chest, the basketball sneakers, runs a manicured nail down the P's looking for Pravdin.

"I'm sorry," she says finally, "but I don't appear to have you on my list."

"Remarkable lady," Pravdin begins, flashing his crooked smile as he edges past the table, "how could you have me on your list when I only just now arrived from the International Symposium on the Inner Ear in Vienna?" Pravdin is past her now, backing toward the dining room. He gives a half bow and turns—to find his path blocked by an unsmiling gorilla with enormous shoulders.

"She said no Pravdin," the gorilla says.

"Listen, friend," Pravdin begins. Peeking around the man he catches a glimpse of Friedemann T. absently popping hors d'oeuvres into his mouth. "What you don't know can hurt you, and what you don't know is who I am."

The gorilla advances; Pravdin retreats toward the street door. "There is no Pravdin," the gorilla repeats.

"Pravdin is what there is," Pravdin retorts. "You have the honor of having him before your very original body. A serious mistake is what you're making. I have friends in high places. I—"

The front door of Aragvi is unceremoniously slammed in his face.

Pravdin, scurrying toward the offices of the All-Union Household Hygiene Bureau, convinces himself that everything that
has happened in the last few days is a coincidence. He reaches
this comforting conclusion by a process of elimination: if it
isn't a coincidence, it's a catastrophe; a catastrophe is unthinkable; ergo, it's a coincidence.

"Three minutes," the man with thick eyeglasses and a
toupee announces, punching his stopwatch and looking up,
lips pursed, at Pravdin.

"Three minutes is all I need," Pravdin launches into his
pitch, "to convince you that vaginal deodorant spray is an
idea whose time has come."

The bureaucrat's jaw droops. "Did I hear you say
vaginal?"

"*Vaginal*, as in *vagina*, is what I said, right. Before you
can build communism you must construct socialism. Before
socialism, an advanced industrial society. And whoever heard
of an advanced industrial society without vaginal deodorant
spray!" Pravdin practically climbs across the desk in excitement; the bureaucrat shrinks back in horror. "Thesis: the
male nostrils, sniffing," Pravdin continues. "Antithesis: the
female organ, pungent. Synthesis:"—Pravdin shouts it out
in a voice raw with lust—"vaginal deodorant spray!"

"Out," orders the bureaucrat, his toupee slipping across
his forehead in agitation. He stabs wildly at intercom buttons
on the desk, yells, "Get him out of here, get him out."
The door is flung open; two burly secretaries advance on
Pravdin, who is packing away the vaginal deodorant spray in
his briefcase. "It comes in three flavors," Pravdin shouts from
the door. "Raspberry, lemon, lime."

"Pervert," screams the bureaucrat, straightening his toupee with both hands as if it is a helmet. "What kind of a man
are you to come in here with this capitalist filth."

"*Homo Economicus* is what kind of man I am," Pravdin yells back, and he makes an obscene gesture with his primitively long, broken, badly set thumb.

Pravdin, thinking about the unthinkable, drops off a Q-Tip at the Department of Medicine at Moscow University, fills in a form requesting that an analysis of its medical potential be prepared for the All-Union Institute for Household Technology.

"I can tell you right off," a lady doctor in a white coat informs Pravdin, "that the shaft is made of wood." She rolls the Q-Tip between her fingers. "The fluffy white stuff at each end is probably cotton. This is an odd bird. What are you supposed to do with it?"

"In the ear is where it goes," Pravdin tells her. "Cleans out wax more efficiently than keys."

The lady doctor frowns. "We have to be careful what goes into the ear, don't we?"

"You're the first person in Russia to suggest that," says Pravdin.

The lady doctor looks up sharply. "I'm not sure I appreciate the implications of that."

Pravdin bristles. "The implication that there is an implication is what I don't appreciate." He slips two Bolshoi tickets into the lady doctor's pocket. "Bewitching lady doctor, I have friends in high places. I could use influence, but I don't take advantage of my name. I wait my turn like any ordinary citizen. An analysis of something that could revolutionize Russia is all I ask."

The lady doctor pockets the Bolshoi tickets. "Russia," she says suspiciously, "has already had its revolution."

With his deformed thumb Pravdin presses the doorbell of the fourth floor apartment off Kutuzovsky Prospect. Instead of the usual buzzer, he hears the distant sound of musical chimes. An eye piece clicks open and Pravdin has the sensation of being sized up; beneath his nonchalance, his skin crawls. Finally, grudgingly, the door is opened a crack—a safety chain prevents it from being opened any wider—and a maid in a starched black uniform with a grim set to her lips stares silently out at him.

"Pravdin, Robespierre Isayevich," Pravdin announces, clicking the heels of his sneakers together, inclining his head, "at your beck and call. Dear lady, I am known to the maestro. I had the honor of obtaining for him two precious tickets to the hockey championship with the Canadians last year."

"Only wait," the maid instructs him, eases shut the door in his face. A few minutes later the door is opened again and Pravdin is ushered through the foyer, the walls and ceiling of which are covered in thick black fabric, into an airy book-lined study. The maestro, wearing blue jeans and a yellow silk robe, his bare feet propped up on his desk, his toes wiggling, sits before a pair of French windows overlooking the Moscow River dictating into a Japanese tape recorder that is voice activated.

"The tape recorder I got you too," Pravdin reminds the maestro. "Also the door chimes."

"Of course I remember you," the Poet says affably. "What can you do for me now?" He laughs at his own joke.

"What I can do for you," Pravdin launches into his pitch, "is add respect to what you already have, which is fame and fortune."

"I am already respected," the Poet says.

"By the wrong people," Pravdin asserts. "Around the bush is where we shouldn't beat. The people who count are the ones who don't read you anymore. The last time you recited your poems, the hall was half full—"

"Three-quarters—"

"Quibble you're not in a position to. The next time you recite, you stick with me, it will be standing room only. Ladies will faint from the lack of oxygen. The ones outside who can't get in will riot." Pravdin leans across the desk, his nose close to the Poet's. "Facts is what we have to confront. Something is missing from your life. Around the age of forty every man comes face to face with the fact that he has not achieved what he thought he would achieve during the period of his optimism; that he is not the man he thought he was. I personally have been spared this because I consider it a major accomplishment, far surpassing my wildest expectations, to be alive at forty. Touch wood. But you, comrade Poet, are another ladleful of yogurt soup. You have the trappings of success: chimes on your door, voice-activated tape recorders and so forth and so on. But respect you don't have. Respect with a capital R is what I'm offering." Pravdin lowers his voice. "A touch of dissidence is what your image needs. Nothing dangerous, naturally, but something to convince the people that all this"—his hand takes in the luxurious apartment behind him—"is what you're prepared to risk when it comes to poetry or principles."

"It goes without saying you have just the issue?"

"If not, here is where I wouldn't be," Pravdin says, sinking back into the chair. "It's this way: I know someone who has written evidence that Honored Artist of the Soviet Union Frolov swiped the manuscript for *The Deep Don* from a White Russian officer named Krukov. Once the original material is made public. Frolov will be *kaput*. It's only a question of who gets the credit for going public."

The Poet stretches his lanky frame. "You don't think the affair is too hot, do you? I have a lecture tour of the United States of America scheduled for next month. New York, Boston, Chicago, Los Angeles. You don't think that would be jeopardized, for instance?"

"The evidence is in black and white," Pravdin assures him. "Frolov has enemies in high places, which is how the manuscript surfaced. On my own I wouldn't be doing this; I'm after all not completely crazy. Exposing Frolov is an idea whose time has come."

"Yes, I see all that," the Poet says thoughtfully. "It only remains, then, to work out what I can do for you in return for bringing me this plum."

Pravdin waves away the idea of payment. "I'm a modest man, maestro, content to store up credit in high places. When you can do me a favor you will know it without my asking."

The Poet rises from the swivel chair suddenly, motions for his visitor to stay where he is, disappears from the study. Pravdin hears a hurried, hushed conversation with the housekeeper, a phone being lifted from its cradle, a door closing, then stillness. He waits five minutes, ten, a quarter of an hour, fidgets with the medals on his Eisenhower jacket, paces. Half an hour goes by and no Poet. Pravdin pokes his head out of the study, spies the housekeeper, her thick arms folded across her breasts, mounting guard on the front door.

"Where, ravishing lady, has our Poet gone to?"

"What Poet?" demands the housekeeper.

"What Poet is a funny question," Pravdin says. He whistles between his teeth, shakes his head. "*The* Poet," he says when the housekeeper makes no reply. "The Poet who sleeps, eats, masturbates, defecates within the wallpapered walls of this faded palace."

"I told you when you forced your way in," the housekeeper says sternly, "he has been on the Black Sea these past two weeks. A mud cure. Maybe now you will believe me."

The man in the blue raincoat and the flat short-brimmed fedora, along with two others in identical raincoats (but bareheaded; Pravdin claims to discern a hierarchy based on whether plainclothes police wear hats) are waiting outside the Poet's apartment building. As Pravdin appears they spring into life. Their movements are precise, choreographed even: one opens the rear door of a black Moskvitch parked at the curb; the other two arrange themselves on either side of Pravdin as if they are parentheses. "You are obliged to come with us," the man with the fedora instructs him.

Pravdin's bloodless lips move, words form but no sound emerges; he is speechless with fear. His tongue goes bone dry, his bowels churn; he passes gas. A neck muscle, then an eyelid, twitches. Infirmities spread through his body like a rash; no sooner has he suppressed one twitch than another pops out. The only proper attitude, it occurs to Pravdin, is panic. Accordingly, his brain loses contact with his knees; his briefcase slips out of his hand; his thin body starts to sag at the joints. The men on either side, experienced in such matters, retrieve the briefcase, catch Pravdin under the armpits and funnel him toward the car.

Pravdin twists his head so that he can see over his shoulder, spots the Poet watching from a fourth-floor window. "Oy, where come with you?" he cries, suddenly finding his voice. "Why come with you?" He tries to catch the eye of a woman pushing a baby carriage, but she walks past as if the little group doesn't exist. "When come with you?" Pravdin croaks, ducking his head and climbing into the back seat. The two blue raincoats pile in after him. "Who are the you I'm supposed to come with?" he whimpers as the door slams shut and the car lurches forward.

The Moskvitch drifts through light traffic back toward the center of Moscow. The man on Pravdin's left takes out a package of American chewing gum, offers a stick to Pravdin. When he doesn't respond, he removes the wrapper and slides it into his mouth. His jaw working, he stares out the window lost in thought. Pravdin presses his nose to the side window, lost in fear. The limousine stops for a red light. Without thinking Pravdin starts to open the door. The man chewing gum gently restrains him.

"Where do you think you're going?"

"Back to nature, if it'll have me," Pravdin replies. Trembling, he coils into a fetal ball in the corner of the back seat.

The car pulls up before the great doors of the KGB complex on Dzerzhinsky Square. Pravdin sees the sidewalk vendor is still there, though the tiny metal wind-up dolls doing military turns have been replaced by wind-up, horse-mounted Don Quixotes with large sombreros and long lances.

The doors swing open, a sentry peers through the driver's window. "Pravdin, Robespierre Isayevich," Pravdin mutters, hoping against hope he'll be told, "There is no Pravdin" and turned away. But the sentry pays no attention to him, instead motions in a stiff-armed military gesture for the car to proceed.

Pravdin is hustled into a windowless, immaculately white, brilliantly lit room with a single stainless steel chair and a stainless steel table.

"Strip," orders a husky attendant. "Clothing on the table, folded."

Under the watchful eyes of the attendant Pravdin unties the laces on his sneakers, pulls them off, then the socks, strips to the skin and folds his Eisenhower jacket and trousers and shirt and underwear on the table. In the neon-bright light his pale skin takes on a sickly yellowish tint. Veins throb in his thin arms. An eye twitches. His head aches. Pravdin brings a hand in a clawing motion to his forehead, presses his damp palm to his clammy skin.

"Bend over, spread your cheeks," orders the attendant. He systematically searches the various openings in Pravdin's body, checks between the toes and behind the ears, runs a fine tooth comb through the wild red hair on his head and the tangled spirally hair on his pubis. Satisfied that Pravdin is hiding nothing, he turns to his clothing and goes over every garment centimeter by centimeter. When he finishes he returns everything except the shoelaces and the belt, indicates with a wave of his hand that Pravdin is to dress, leads him into another room that looks like a doctor's waiting room. There are several old chairs with worn fabric, a pile of Polish magazines on a low table, a window with a wire mesh grille on the outside overlooking Dzerzhinsky Square and the Detsky Mir, a toy emporium across the way. The glass on the window is thick, the window is screwed shut, and the sounds of the traffic are very faint, almost as if they originate in Pravdin's memory.

Pravdin fogs up the glass with his breath, writes on the fog with his deformed thumb:

Chopping off heads is infectious—one today, another
tomorrow and what will be left of the Party?

(I. Stalin: Pravdin figures this came from the horse's mouth), hears someone at the door, erases the graffiti with his sleeve just as he is summoned for interrogation.

He is led through a maze of corridors and steel staircases to a room with an unmarked pale green door. With a flick of his head the guard motions Pravdin inside.

Inside he goes—to find himself staring at the lidded eyes, the shiny bald head, the tiny nostrils, the thin feminine lips of the Druse, Chuvash Al-hakim bi'amrillahi. Again Pravdin's bloodless lips move, again words form, again no sound emerges; he is speechless with bewilderment. The Druse indicates with the forefinger of his right hand against his lips that Pravdin is to remain silent; he indicates with his eyes that the walls have ears; he indicates with two fingers of his left hand that Pravdin is to take the only other seat in the room.

"I am called Melor," the Druse begins. He lights an American filter-tip cigarette from the butt of an old one. "I will pose to you certain questions"—he taps with the long nail of his pinky a dossier open on the desk in front of him—"which have already been composed. You will think a moment and reply. We will now start." The Druse studies the dossier, coughs discreetly into a silk handkerchief, switches on a tape recorder. "You were expelled from Lomonosov University for antisocialist onanism. You are now rumored to be involved in group sexual activities. Is that accurate?"

"Group sexual activities is what I would love to be involved in," Pravdin cries passionately. "With me, two is already a crowd, one is unfortunately par. And where explain me is the law against masturbation?"

"Our interest is not so much in the sexual activities of the group, but in the existence of the group for whatever reason. A group is a place where conspiracies incubate."

"*Participes curarum* is the only group I've ever belonged to," claims Pravdin.

"What language is that, Jewish?"

"Jewish is right," says Pravdin. "It's an old Talmudic expression that means, 'sharers of troubles.' "

The Druse puts a tick next to an item in the dossier. "To move on, you are said to have attempted to bribe a woman at the Housing Ministry with two tickets to a performance at the Bolshoi of"—he glances at his notes—"*Eugene Onegin.*"

"*Tosca* is what it was. I left the tickets in my papers by mistake," Pravdin explains lamely. "I asked for them back. Give them to me is what she wouldn't do."

Another tick. "You were seen walking on the grass in Sokolniki Park."

"There was no sign that said keep off."

"Keep off is understood."

"Not by me. Detailed instructions are what I need."

Another tick. "You obviously have a certain strength that originates in your lack of character; perhaps we should call it 'strength of character-less-ness.' It occurs to me that that accounts for why it is difficult to categorize you. You don't seem to fit anywhere."

"I'm easy to categorize," Pravdin says. "Afraid is what I am."

"Everyone's afraid," comments the Druse.

"You even?"

The Druse smiles weakly. "I'm afraid that one day I'll come face to face with someone who won't be afraid. To continue: You were observed meeting on several occasions with the American journalist Graham Hull. What was talked about?"

"The advances, touch wood, that have been made under scientific socialism," Pravdin explains. "The inevitable victory of the working classes. Alienation. Vanguard of the proletariat. Withering away of the state. Surplus capital. And so forth and so on."

"What are Q-Tips? Classic comics? Red Army exercises? Instant matzos? What is a vaginal deodorant spray?"

"Q-Tips are an idea whose time has come." Pravdin launches into his pitch. Firing from the hip in short bursts, he explains each of the items on the Druse's list. "Thesis: the male nostril, sniffing. Antithesis: the female organ, pungent. Synthesis: vaginal deodorant spray!" Leaning across the desk until his face is only centimeters from the Druse's, he hisses: "Crazy is what I am!"

"That possibility is being considered," the Druse replies evenly. He takes another sheet of paper from the dossier, studies it as he lights a new cigarette. "Explain, if you can, the significance of the following: *Quis custodiet ipsos custodes;* I've seen the future and it needs work; Nothing worth knowing can be taught; To dine with the devil use a long spoon; Behind every fortune is a crime; Full conformity is possible only in the cemetery; The shortage shall be divided among the peasants; Publish *and* perish; So here it is at last, the Distinguished Thing; and last but by no means least, Chopping off heads is infectious—one today, another tomorrow and what will be left of the Party." The Druse looks up, winks at Pravdin. "I believe we missed only one: you wrote something with a fingertip in the air. My operatives would have gotten it except for the fact that you weren't working in Cyrillic."

"French was the language of the moment," Pravdin informs him. "My thumb, not my finger, is what I used. *Jesus, sauve Toi* is what I wrote."

"*Jesus, sauve Toi*," the Druse adds in longhand to his list. "Thank you. Would you now comment on the significance of these phrases."

"Graffiti is what they are," Pravdin explains. "Steam is what I'm letting off. It's this way: I was wounded in the war. Shrapnel in the neck. Pinched nerve. The ability to shrug is what I lost. Result: tensions build up in me. Frustrations that others shrug away in me poison the blood, pinch the bladder, constrict the solar plexus; When I pass gas it's always half an octave lower than anyone else out of nervousness. The only way I can live normally is to work off my frustrations. So I scribble on walls, windows, the sky even."

"Graffiti is antisocialist," the Druse informs him, "and out of place in a country that prides itself on progress. You do see that we are a land of progress, don't you?"

"A land of progress is what we definitely are," Pravdin readily agrees. "With my own eyes I've witnessed it. Take for example Uzbekistan, where shepherds pitch their *yurtas* around a six horsepower transformer with leads into each tent to watch color TV on large screens. It's enough to take your breath away."

"Just so," the Druse agrees tonelessly.

Pravdin scribbles a note, passes it to the Druse. It says:

"When can I see you?" Out loud, he asks: "Why have I been brought here for interrogation?"

"You were picked up at random when your number came up in our computer."

"My detention has nothing to do with . . . nothing?"

"Absolutely routine," the Druse assures him.

"Manuscripts you're not interested in?"

"What manuscripts are you talking about?" the Druse inquires.

"I'm writing a social history of the shrug," Pravdin declares. " 'The Shrug as Antithesis' is its working title."

The Druse shrugs to indicate his lack of interest.

"And I can go?" Pravdin whispers.

The Druse passes Pravdin a note that says: "Sandunovsky Bath House at ten." Out loud, he says: "You can go, yes."

Pravdin lifts his body off the seat as if it were bruised, backs toward the door, expecting at any moment the floor to give way beneath his sneakers, sending him spinning into some dark snakepit of a cell for twelve more years. To his astonishment the floor remains solidly beneath his feet. He reaches out and puts a hand on the knob and gingerly turns it, certain it will be locked. To his astonishment the door clicks open. He turns back to the Druse. "One question is what I have," he says.

"Only ask."

"Melor is not a name I've come across before. Russian it doesn't sound. What is its origin, if it doesn't offend you my asking?"

"Melor," said the Druse, "is an acronym for Marx, Engels, Lenin, Organizers of Revolution."

CHAPTER 7

The sidewalk vendor is down to
his last wind-up Quixote . . .

The sidewalk vendor is down to his last wind-up Quixote when Pravdin emerges into the thickening dusk, which is gathering over Moscow like the folds of a fire curtain. A sullen child with jutting ears silently pulls his reluctant mother toward the doll, which wheels on its horse and jerkily charges, lance level, a cardboard windmill.

"Want, want," whines the child, tugging at his mother's miniskirt until it comes off her hip. "Want."

"How much?" the mother demands, annoyed at the vendor for putting temptation in her son's way.

"Four rubles," the vendor replies.

"Four rubles!" The woman is incredulous.

"Want, want," cries the boy.

"Wanting is antisocialist," Pravdin whispers in the woman's ear. "Don Quixote also. Attention: those who are not with us are considered to be against us." He shakes his head with exaggerated sadness. "Besides which, the windmill is who always wins."

"For you, three rubles fifty," the vendor coaxes.

"Want, want," cries the child.

The woman looks at Pravdin as if he has bad breath, spins on one stiletto heel and wobbles off, yanking the boy after her so suddenly that he is lifted clear off the earth and trails after her like the tail of a kite.

The sidewalk vendor turns on Pravdin a look so mournful that he knows he is being hustled. He fishes from his change purse three rubles fifty, offers it to the vendor.

"Four rubles," the vendor begs.

"Three fifty is what it was a minute ago," complains Pravdin.

"For you, four," the vendor stands firm.

Pravdin reluctantly counts out the change from his purse. The vendor accepts payment, verifies it. Pravdin, frustrated by his inability to shrug, stuffs the Don Quixote into his bulging briefcase, starts off in the direction of the Sandunovsky Bath House. Head angled into a gale that isn't blowing, he crosses the cobblestones of Red Square, looks up to check his wristwatches against the great clock in the Kremlin tower, notices workmen draping from the Kremlin wall the first huge May Day banners, sees the minute hand of the great clock moving as if it is a second hand, sees the hour hand making the rounds as if it is a minute hand. Not at all dismayed, Pravdin turns his attention to a water truck making its way across the cobblestones directly toward a well-dressed men carrying a sack of avocados. Neither truck nor man veer. The truck escalates; its sprinkling system douses the cobblestones for five meters on either side. Pravdin, fearful the truck will turn on him, dances away from an attack not made. The man with the avocados retreats too—too late, too late. His feet disappear in a swell of water. Pravdin, still reeling from his session with the Druse, has the impression that the well-dressed man, avocados held high to keep them dry, is walking on water, and he stares at the scene as if it is an epiphany.

"Epiphanies," an inner voice warns him, "are antisocialist."

"Those who are not with us," Pravdin mutters out loud, "are considered to be off their rockers."

"Talking to yourself," Pravdin consoles himself, "has this advantage: conspiracy you can't be accused of."

"My kingdom," Pravdin moans, "for a shrug."

In frustration he scrawls in chalk across the inside of the Kremlin wall:

Better fewer, but better

(V. Lenin: Pravdin has a passion for quality control), dodges between some Scandinavian tourists staring up at the golden dome of an Orthodox church, zigs down several alleyways to make sure he isn't being followed, continues at a more leisurely pace in the direction of the Sandunovsky Bath House.

Inside the entrance Pravdin counts out sixty kopecks, hands the change to an emaciated man sitting stiffly on a stool behind a high wooden counter. Pravdin senses that something is not quite right with the man, but it takes him several seconds of staring before he can put his finger on it: the ticket taker doesn't appear to be breathing. Without any visible vital life signs except a tired mechanical muscular motion, he drops the kopecks into a compartmented drawer, tears off a ticket from a reel of tickets, rips it in half and deposits both halves in a cardboard box already brimming with torn

tickets. Pravdin helps himself to a rough white sheet from a
pile stacked on a chair, strips quickly in the change room
warm with the smell of sweat and birch bark, drapes the sheet
across his shoulder like a toga, tips the attendant to keep an
eye on his briefcase and change purse, skips the ritual weigh-
ing-in, enters the steam room. Instantly the hot moist air
burns his nostrils, stings his eyes. Blinking quickly, gasping for
air, Pravdin almost collides with a man sucking on a piece of
salted fish. Another man with "For Stalin and the Motherland" tattooed on his biceps dashes a bucketful of water onto
the fire bricks. Steam hisses off them into the saturated air.
Wooden benches lined with naked, coughing men gradually
come into view—a landfall seen through steam! Pravdin peers
through the clouds of swirling steam looking for circumcised
penises, spots none, keeps his toga draped casually over his
private parts as he takes a vacant place on the end of a bench.

Next to him a pink-skinned man flails away at his back
with a bouquet of leafy birch twigs, clears his throat several
times, calls across the room in a commanding voice for someone to pour more water on the fire bricks, turns to Pravdin
and out of the blue says: "Russia is a mysterious country, if
you want my opinion."

"Give me a for instance," demands Pravdin.

"For instance," the pink-skinned man obliges, "in all of
Russia there is no place to get trousers cuffed, but millions
upon millions of men are walking around with cuffs on their
trousers."

"Cuffs," Pravdin mumbles, "are a covenant between God
and his chosen people."

"God is dead," the pink-skinned man says gently.

"Touch wood," Pravdin replies, rapping his knuckles on
the bench.

The pink-skinned man leans toward Pravdin; his head
emerges out of the steam, but not his body, causing Pravdin

to imagine that the two are no longer connected, assuming they ever were. "Tell me the truth," he asks Pravdin, "you don't really like steam, do you?"

"You read minds too," he remarks sourly.

The pink-skinned man retreats into the steam; his voice, mocking in tone, emerges as if filtered by some barely remembered grievance. "The mister you want to see also doesn't like steam. You can not like steam together in a private room, the door of which is behind you and to your right."

Walking as casually as his throbbing pulse will allow, Pravdin makes his way to the door in question, tries the knob, peeks in to see the Druse, Chuvash Al-hakim bi'amrillahi, stretched out naked on a medical table under a sunlamp. His eyes are protected by small dark goggles; his tanned body, which has no hair that Pravdin can see (even around his organ), is covered with squirming bloodsuckers that an old myopic woman tends, murmuring to them in a language Pravdin doesn't recognize, rubbing their spinal columns with the coarse tip of her forefinger until they are erect and bloated. Sitting on a stool behind the Druse's head is Zosima, the Berber girl with the small blue flower tattooed on one cheek. (Pravdin could swear it was on her left side the last time he saw her; now it is on her right cheek.) She is reading in soft, rhythmic Arabic from a large book open in her lap, the epic *Manas*. Chuvash rolls his eyes slowly in the direction of the slightly open door, senses that Pravdin is there before he catches sight of him. "*Salaam aleikum*, brother."

Pravdin is tempted to back away, to flee, but he reasons that a discussion with the Druse is an idea whose time has long since come. Pulling his toga tightly around him, he enters (on clenched toes; the marble floor is ice) as if he is stepping into a Greek tragedy. "*Shalom Aleichem* back to you," he says, bowing awkwardly, deeply, hoping to hide the

awkwardness in the deepness, hoping to convey by the deepness an impression of irony.

"Can I offer you some bloodsuckers?" the Druse inquires politely. "A purge of blood every three days is said to
increase stamina, cleanse the brain, stimulate the intuition,
which is the essential element in social intercourse."

Pravdin declines the offer with a brisk wave of his hand.
"Thanks to you but no thanks to you," he says. "Bloodsuckers are what I deal with all day."

Chuvash says something in Azerbaijanian to the old
woman; she switches off the sunlamp, plucks leeches from
his body, drops them with soft splashes into a large jar three-
quarters full of water. One by one they sink to the bottom.
Zosima closes her book; the old woman caps the jar and the
two of them slip from the room through a curtain that
hides another door. The Druse motions Pravdin to Zosima's
seat but he stubbornly refuses to take it, instead circles slowly
the table on which the Druse, goggleless, now sits in an un-
flawed lotus position.

"What name, if it doesn't upset your red corpuscle
balance my posing the question, do I call you by?" Pravdin
points at the Druse with his deformed thumb. "Who are you
is what I'm asking?"

The Druse's thumb and forefinger float slowly toward
his face, settle over the eyelids, guide them down over his
eyes, remain resting like weights on the lashes. His lips
drift into a quizzical half smile. "I am Chuvash Al-hakim
bi'amrillahi, a male by sex, a Druse by religion. I believe, like
all Druses, that the soul passes after death into new incarnations of greater perfection. I believe, like all Druses, there is
one and only one God, indefinable, incomprehensible, inef-
fable, passionless, who has made Himself known to man by
seventy successive incarnations, including the Jew, Jesus, but
excluding Muhammed. I believe the most recent incarna-

tion was the sixth Fatimite Caliph of Egypt, Al-hakim bi'-amrillahi, after whom I am called. I believe I am the sixth Fatimite Caliph of Egypt, who disappeared in the year anno Domini 1021, reincarnated; I believe I am the seventy-first incarnation of God, come to open again to the faithful the door of mercy, come to conquer Mecca and Jerusalem, come to convince the world of the inevitability of the Faith, come to demand obedience to the seven commandments of Hamza, my vizier in my previous incarnation, the first and greatest of which requires truth in words—but only when Druse speaks to Druse."

Pravdin sinks into Zosima's chair. "And non-Druses?" he asks weakly. "What of us?"

Chuvash continues to give the impression he is reciting chapter and verse. "A Druse may say what he pleases to a non-Druse, so long as he, the Druse, doesn't raise his voice, so long as he keeps the secrets of the Faith, so long as he abstains from wine and tobacco, so long as he wears no gold or silver."

"You tripped up!" Pravdin points an accusing finger. "When you were Melor, you chain-smoked like a chimney. Explain away that if you can."

Chuvash is unperturbed. "Druses have permission to conform outwardly to the faith of the unbelievers among whom they dwell."

"Even the seventy-first incarnation of God?"

"Especially the seventy-first incarnation of God," the Druse replies. "If God doesn't conform, who will?"

"The Jew, Jesus, didn't conform," Pravdin notes sourly.

"The Jew, Jesus, finished his earthly mission nailed to a cross. I intend to conquer Mecca and Jerusalem, open again to the faithful the door of mercy, convince the world of the inevitability of the Faith, demand obedience to the seven commandments of—"

"Off your rocker is what you are," Pravdin cuts him off. "Not one word of this is what I believe. But as a lady friend of mine says, that's another story." Pravdin leans forward, taps a finger on the Druse's knee. "What I want to know—"

Chuvash interrupts with a gesture indicating the walls have ears.

"If ears are what the walls have," cries Pravdin, "stuff them full of cotton is what a sane person would do, or better still pierce the inner ears with things they don't want to hear and make them deaf. Who's listening anyhow? Melor is listening is who's listening. But who is Melor? The Druse, Chuvash Al-hakim bi'amrillahi, in another incarnation maybe? And what does this Marx-Engels-Lenin-Organizers-Revolution want with a Jewish hustler like me? Answer me that if you can. And why does Chuvash arrange for me an apartment in the last wooden house in central Moscow and Melor have me followed so he knows every word I scribble on a wall? Is Chuvash trying to encourage me to expose a literary fraud, and Melor trying to intimidate me so that I lay off? A sane person could be confused by all this. A crazy person too."

"We are all of us," the Druse explains patiently, "many people. I am just more open, or formal if you like, about it. Melor is one of the hats it suits me to wear to accomplish what I intend to accomplish, which is to open again to the faithful the door of mercy, conquer Mecca and Jerusalem, convince the world of the inevitability—"

"All this is what you've said already," Pravdin interrupts impatiently. "Enough of this religious bla-bla-bla. Explain what's what and who's who."

Chuvash slips from the table, takes a white silk sheet from the shelf beneath it, winds it around himself, moves the chair the old myopic woman used so that it faces Pravdin. "You have a right to an explanation, I am ready to concede you that," he begins.

"Me too, I'm ready to concede me that," Pravdin agrees dejectedly.

"As Chuvash, I brought the girl Nadezhda, the woman known as Mother Russia and you together in the last wooden house in central Moscow, and then dropped the manuscripts in your collective laps because I represent people in high places who want to ruin Honored Artist of the Soviet Union Frolov. Or to be more precise, they want to ruin one very important person on the Politburo who has protected Frolov against charges of plagiarism all these years. As Melor, I became aware that you were about to come into possession of manuscripts that could ruin Honored Artist of the Soviet Union Frolov, thereby compromising the position of his protector on the Politburo, who happens to be my client as well as my superior. I therefore took immediate steps to monitor your conversations, keep track of your activities, record the messages you wrote on various walls, any one of which could have been a coded signal to the agent who was providing you with the manuscripts."

"But you are the agent who provided me with the manuscripts!"

"Just so," the Druse agrees.

"Oy. How can you play two people at once is what I don't understand," Pravdin squeals, unable to control his voice. "Schizophrenic is what you have to be."

The Druse is not amused. "It is difficult to grasp, I can see that, how one person can represent two constituencies that have conflicting interests. At heart, I suppose, it is a matter of self-discipline. It is very much like playing chess with yourself, which is something I do every evening after I meditate. First I am white, and I move the king's pawn forward two spaces in order to develop my king's bishop. Then I am black. I know white has opened with his king's pawn because he intends to develop his king's bishop, so I forestall that by moving my queen's pawn forward two spaces. Then I am white again, and I know that black has divined my intention to develop my king's bishop, so I—"

"Playing like that you could go insane," Pravdin explains. "Listening to you *I* could go insane."

"It is every bit as difficult as it sounds," the Druse concedes, "but I am convinced that with practice any normal person could do it. As Chuvash, for instance, I am absolutely sure that you are in full control of your faculties, which is to say, that you are perfectly sane. As Melor, on the other hand, I am beginning to have honest doubts on the matter." Chuvash shrugs apologetically.

"That makes me the modern existential hero," Pravdin mutters, "the man in the middle. What do I do now is the question I'm asking? Which voice do I listen to, Chuvash's or Melor's?"

"You listen to your own voice," Chuvash suggests. "If you really are the modern existential hero, then you have absolute freedom of choice. Your problem is to find a rational criterion to serve as a basis for making this choice, a task you find difficult, if not impossible, because you are convinced in the utter absurdity of the world in which you function, and hence in the absurdity of making the effort to make a rational choice. Your problem is to rise above the absurdity and act, either as Chuvash tells you to or as Melor tells you to."

"What if Melor decides to put the screws on? What if?"

"Chuvash will know about it beforehand, will warn you, will do his best to protect you."

"Who will win this tug-of-war is what I want to know, white or black?"

"It doesn't matter who wins," Chuvash says. "The only thing that counts is to play."

Pravdin shakes his head in confusion, blows his nose into a corner of his toga, moves (flat-footed; the marble floor is still ice but his mind is elsewhere) toward the door. "It is only fair telling you," he informs Melor, who stares after him with an appraising eye, "that the microphone in the table leg is what I found the day I moved into the attic."

Melor accepts this with a nod. "The microphone you found," he tells Pravdin, "was the one you were supposed to find so you wouldn't look for others."

Pravdin passes through the steam, skips the ritual weighing-out, dresses quickly with his back to the room to hide his covenant with a God in whom he doesn't believe, retrieves his briefcase from the attendant, removes the change purse from the briefcase, checks to make sure the money is all there, finds in the coin compartment an entrance pass to the Writers' Congress that starts the next day. "Chuvash," he tries to figure it out, "had this put here, which means that Melor knows I have it, which means that Chuvash knows that Melor knows I have it. Oy"—his palm slaps against his high forehead in exasperation—"insanity may be an idea whose time has come. Touch wood." And his knuckles rap without conviction against the wooden bench.

Sequences flicker before Pravdin's eyes like frames from an old Eisenstein. Eyeglasses shatter; the baby carriage hurtles down the steps. Pravdin has always been curious who was in that carriage. Now he knows! One moment he is outside the carriage watching it career out of control with its terror-stricken baby cargo. The next *he is inside the carriage*, curled up in a fetal position, sucking desperately on his deformed thumb, feeling the bouncing wheels jar his bruised spine, hearing the pitch of the panicky screams rise and fall as he streaks past the source of the sound. Oy, his tiny palm slaps against his tiny forehead, it's *me* inside. Baby Robespierre pulls back on his erect joy stick as the carriage picks up speed;

it soars into the sky, wheeling in a great arc over Moscow. Comfortably airborne, he grips the side of the carriage and peers over the edge, feels the wind fill his bonnet, sees far below huge crowds funneling into Red Square for the May Day parade. On a whim he begins to fart a stream of smoke and skywrites over Red Square:

Waak, waak, Honored Artist of
the Soviet Union Frolov is a plagiarist

Instantly Melor's voice crackles over the radio: "What language is that, Jewish?" he demands. "Jewish is right," Baby Robespierre explains. "It's an old Talmudic saying that means, it's me who will watch the bosses." He burps diabolically into the microphone, freezes in fear when dozens of balls of cotton begin bursting around the carriage. The seventy-first burst explodes just underneath and rocks the carriage; flames spurt from the sides and it starts to spiral toward the ground which, impatient for the crash, rushes up to meet it.

"Aiiiiiiiii!" screams Pravdin, bolting upright in bed, sweaty and weak and wide awake. Nadezhda, looking around wildly, bolts upright too, absorbs what's happening, presses her palm to his wet forehead, eases him back on the pillow, stroking all the while his forehead and, as he calms down and breathes more regularly, his penis, which slowly becomes erect.

Their lovemaking is a triumph of sex over terror. Gradually the shattered eyeglasses, the carriage hurtling down the steps, the bursts of cotton, the ground spiraling up to meet him, lose their narrative thread; Pravdin clings to the broken images as if they are buoys, but Nadezhda descends on his erection with silent lips, draws it slowly into her mouth, strokes it with a tongue as roughly caressing as a cat's. Pravdin relinquishes the dream, lets it slip through his fingers, moans, tries to pull free when he feels himself coming off —too late, too late. Nadezhda locks him in her with her hand

and accepts his flow, which seems to originate from some center so deep inside him he has never conceded its existence.

"Aiiiiiiii," Pravdin stifles a cry in the pillow as she sucks the last drops from him—a pleasure so close to pain he thinks he will go crazy if she stops or if she doesn't.

When he finally musters enough force to speak, Pravdin's voice is hoarse. "I tell you—" he says. He closes his eyes and sits motionless for a long moment. "I tell you," he begins again, "that lovemaking makes the time stand still for me. You think a moment, reply, 'Pleasure is a clock like any other.' "

"What a cynical thing for me to say," Nadezhda writes. "I look old but I talk young."

They sleep again, Nadezhda tossing restlessly, Pravdin deep into a dreamless pit from which he has trouble emerging when it grows gray. At breakfast Mother Russia lays out yogurts, wheat germ cereal, a steaming bowl of Lapsang Suchong made from teabags Nadezhda picked up from a diplomat's wife in exchange for some photographs of her children.

"I got off another zinger to Singer," Zoya informs them conversationally. "This one's a time bomb. I told him people in an industrial society lose a sense of who they are and begin to see themselves as others see them, which is why we are all of us so different depending on whom we are with. I also told him I was an observer but only in the sense that his fellow American A. Toklas was an observer, which is to say she liked a view but she liked to sit with her back turned to it. I told him that that was the only way to look at things and stay sane."

"If you sit with your back turned," complains Pravdin, "you can't see where you're going."

"Even with your back not turned," Zoya argues, "you can't see where you're going. Anatole France, who was a charming sentimentalist before his tongue turned acid, once said something about how the future was hidden from the men who make it. To which I say, thanks God. If they could see where they were going they'd lose interest in the trip."

"The future," writes Nadezhda, "is like seeing yourself in a mirror with your hair parted on the wrong side."

"Every time I look in a mirror," Pravdin remarks, "nobody is whom I half expect to see looking back." He smiles self-consciously. "Up to now there's always been somebody: me with my medals on the wrong side of my Eisenhower jacket. Touch wood." (His knuckles rap on the kitchen table.)

"There aren't many people left who touch wood," observes Zoya.

"There aren't many people left who have wood to touch," says Pravdin.

"Not funny," groans Zoya.

"Not meant to be," replies Pravdin.

"People don't touch wood," explains Zoya, "because they're no longer superstitious. The decline of superstition, if you want my opinion, is one of the tragedies of our epoch. If you are interested in the why, it's because psychoanalysis has occupied the ground it left vacant. The social unit of the future, if there is a future, will be the Therapeutic State in which the principal requirement for the position of Big Brother will be an M.D. degree. Ha! Those medical Attilas, with their ugly little hearts contorted like fists, will run the world as if it were one long umbilical ward."

"*Waak, waak, power to the powerful, power to the powerful,*" comes from Mother Russia's bedroom.

"If I had to bet," Nadezhda writes, "I'd bet the future will be futureless."

"Not funny," Pravdin scribbles on her napkin.

"Not meant to be," she prints, in all capitals, under his scrawl.

Zoya regards Pravdin with a mixture of shrewdness and affection. "Our new attic reminds me more and more of my late, silly, beautiful husband. An idealism just beyond articulation illuminated his actions the way cities over the horizon light up the night sky long before you actually see them."

"Idealism is an ideal," protests Pravdin, "not a formula for everyday survival."

"You tried that out on me already," Zoya chides him. "I didn't believe you then, I don't believe you now. You're a closet idealist."

Pravdin wipes the wheat germ off his chin with his hand, adds milk to his tea, blows on it, bends his head down to the glass and noisily sips. "What you want to see, little mother, you see. When I was young, a problem child is what I was: Narcissus, Onan and Oedipus rolled into one. A problem man is what I grew into. In summer I used to haunt the banks of the Moscow River looking for lovers who swam naked, then swiped the clothes they left on the banks. The thefts were never reported because the militia frowned on naked swimming and advertise is what people didn't do."

Nadezhda, preoccupied with dark thoughts, absently stuffs into her carryall an old Leica, two lenses, spare film, her wallet, a notebook with measurements of all her friends (if she comes across hard-to-get items of clothing, she will buy for everyone), starts for the door, changes her mind, comes marching back, writes with determination on her pad: "Enough is enough. For God's sake give them the manuscripts and be done with it."

"You're off your rocker," says Pravdin, pushing the note away.

"What did I say," Zoya cries jubilantly. "A closet idealist! You light up the night sky from over the horizon." She scrapes her chair closer to Pravdin's, takes in her wrinkled fingers the lapel of his Eisenhower jacket, whispers urgently: "Unarmed truth can defeat even the seventy-first incarnation of God."

"*Waak, waak, power to the powerful, power to the powerful.*" The bird lands on the bowl of fruit on top of the refrigerator, preens, pleased with its short flight. "*Waak, waak.*"

"The Writers' Congress is the perfect platform," Zoya insists confidently. "Confront them with the facts, they'll have to listen." Her eyes become watery with excitement. Her fingers cling weakly to his lapel. She says harshly: "What are Chuvash and Melor against the likes of you. Confuse them is all you have to do. Become two personages yourself: one who wants to drop the whole thing and give back the manuscripts; the other a stubborn bastard who walks on water, moves mountains, works up a sweat from a noneconomic activity!"

"Two personages is what I am already," Pravdin announces morbidly. "I'm the hustler and the hustled." He is frustrated by his inability to shrug; this would be the perfect moment. "Schizophrenia is an idea whose time has obviously come."

Nadezhda shakes her head angrily, writes, "Two can be arrested as cheaply as one," drops the note in Pravdin's plate, stalks from the kitchen.

Pravdin pushes away the plate as if it contains a bill he doesn't want to pay, grabs a pepper grinder and thrusts it in front of Mother Russia's mouth. "In your opinion, Zoya Aleksandrovna, what is the most important problem facing the world today?"

Mother Russia responds instantly. "Ha!" she cackles, "that's deliciously simple: it's population control. If you ask me, the government should drape the Kremlin with giant posters that say, 'Have Cats, Not Brats.' Between you, me and the wall, who are the three listening to my every word, Hemingway is the only cat lover in all of history I loathe. But that's another story."

"Waak, waak, help, help," barks Pravdin. But his sinking heart isn't in the game.

Pravdin, cooling his heels on a wooden bench with initials carved all over it, stares at the small hand-lettered sign ("Department of Medicine, Moscow University") until the letters blur and he loses a sense of where he is, who he is even.

"Pravdin, Robespierre Isayevich," an inner voice reminds him, "Homo Economicus with a jackpot mentality, hustler with the instincts of a victim, gate-crasher with a taste for black Beluga, graffitist who can turn watchstraps into sandals but not water into wine, shrugless in Gaza, a light sleeper and a heavy dreamer, no closet anything, vaguely aware of a covenant with God but suspicious that the Party of the First Part is not holding up His end of the Deal, and so forth and so on."

He suspends the inventory, glances at his two wristwatches, sees he's been waiting already two hours, carves with a small pocketknife in the wooden bench:

Patience is a form of despair

(Anon: Pravdin has spent the better part of his life despairing). Twenty minutes later the report Pravdin has come for is presented to him by a secretary. It says:

Analysis of a cotton toothpick, prepared under the auspices of the Department of Medicine, Moscow University.

1. The cotton toothpick consists of a sliver of wood, eight centimeters in length, with tufts of cotton weighing approximately .07 gram, glued to each end.

2. With respect to the proposal to use the cotton toothpick to

remove wax from the concha area of the ear, the following points should be taken into consideration:

a. while it is considered possible to remove the wax with the implement under analysis,

b. certain risks are involved, most notably the possibility of damage to the internal auditory meatus or a puncture of the inner ear caused by too profound insertion of the cotton toothpick.

3. Conclusion: While wax-free ears are considered desirable in an advanced industrial society, they are clearly not indispensable. Furthermore, the presence of the wax does not constitute in itself a sufficient health hazard to warrant running risks to remove it. In severe cases, when quantities of wax are allowed to build up, a slight infringement of auditory ability has resulted. This can be overcome by:

a. turning up the volume of the sound source.

b. removing the wax with traditional methods, i.e. keys, fingernails (only women's nails are considered sufficiently long for this purpose), which have lower risk quotients than the cotton toothpick in question.

> Prepared, this date
> by A. N. Kulakova,
> candidate examiner,
> eyes, ears, nose, throat
> and sexual problems section.
>
> Reviewed and approved,
> this date, by N. R.
> Prornik, chief of section,
> eyes, ears, nose, throat
> and sexual problems.

"What's this sudden lust for traditional methods," Pravdin explodes, tapping the sheet with the back of his hand. The secretary, a matronly woman in a white coat two sizes too large for her, backs away. "What do they do for fun in the eyes, ears, nose, throat and sexual problems section," Pravdin yells after her, "swab throats with skeleton keys? Conduct gynecological examinations with the back of soup spoons?" A maniacal look comes into his eyes and he hefts his briefcase as if he is about to use it as a weapon. The woman cowers inside her white coat, turns her shoulder and peers at him over it.

"No offense meant," she says softly, "but you're crazy."

"Ha!" cries Pravdin, dancing menacingly back and forth across her field of vision. "Under capitalism, man exploits man. Yes or maybe?" His rust hair flies off in all directions, giving to him the appearance of an agitated conductor. He scrapes what he can from an ear with a fingernail and thrusts it under her nose. "Nothing is what you remove from an ear with a fingernail," he screams. "Nothing is *no thing*."

Two interns in white coats escort him from the building. "Temper is what anybody can lose," Pravdin explains as they push him into the revolving door, rotate the panels, spill him into the street. Pravdin straightens his Eisenhower jacket, adjusts the four medals overlapping on his breast, brushes off non-existent lint from his sleeves, moistens a finger with saliva and writes on the glass wall of the entrance to the university:

IF NOT I, WHO?

IF NOT NOW, WHEN?

(Anon: Pravdin has a flash image of himself as a Bedouin-robed Old Testament Isaiah anticipating the coming of the Suffering Servant). The two interns read what Pravdin has written, look at each other, start toward the revolving door, but he skips away into the crowd and disappears.

Red Square is cordoned off by police barriers; peasant women in layers of dark clothing are beginning to scrub down the cobblestones for the May Day pass in review. The buildings on Gorky Street, in the other direction, are draped with giant red banners, each containing some bit of socialist graffiti. "High moral qualities are the bricks with which we build Communism," proclaims one. Another says, "Peace" in fourteen languages. Pravdin drifts into a group of Bulgarians snapping pictures of Red Square over the barrier, interests one in a Swiss watch that registers seconds, minutes, hours and the phases of the moon.

"How much?" the tourist demands, testing the expanding band.

"Not for sale," Pravdin mumbles. "For trade."

"What do I have that you want?" the Bulgarian asks in puzzlement.

"The ability to shrug," whines Pravdin, snatches back the watch, dances away toward the main offices of the All-Soviet Proletarian Savings Bank.

"If you want to open an account," snaps the thin man behind an enormous desk, looking up reluctantly from his papers, "it's window seven."

"Settling accounts, not opening them, is what I'm interested in," Pravdin explains, advancing on the man like a lava flow, depositing his briefcase on his desk. "It's this way: Socialism has done so much for me, I want to return the principal with the interest. So I'm here to give you a new twist to the savings game, something into which you could branch." Pravdin takes a deep breath, leans forward, speaks confidentially. "Sperm banks are an idea whose time has come. Before you can build communism you must construct socialism. Before socialism, an advanced industrial society. And who ever heard of an advanced industrial society without sperm banks!" Pravdin climbs across the desk in excitement. "Thesis: overpopulation. Antithesis: vasectomies. Synthesis:" Pravdin shouts it out in a weary voice "sperm banks, where men can deposit their seeds in case they have second thoughts."

The thin man behind the desk stabs wildly at the intercom buttons. A woman, then a uniformed guard, then two other men, come running. "Get him out of here!" the thin man cries hysterically.

"A deposit is all I wanted to make," pleads Pravdin, shrinking back against a wall, protecting his crotch with his briefcase.

"You should be in an asylum," the thin man yells after him as the four employees escort him toward the exit.

"I am already," Pravdin flings over his shoulder, "is what the problem is."

Pravdin, the collar of his Eisenhower jacket turned up against a chill that isn't in the air, huddles in a doorway across the street from the Writers' Congress auditorium. Traffic thins out. Street lights come on. He starts to cross the street, tiptoeing around pools of light as if he is trying to avoid getting his basketball sneakers wet, when Friedemann T. rushes out of the night.

"Be a good fellow, don't say hello before I speak, don't say good-bye after I finish, only listen with both your ears," he instructs Pravdin, holding up a pudgy palm to silence him. "I was told I would find you here, which is how come our paths cross. I was told to tell you only this: Return the originals, burn the photocopy, and an exit visa for Israel will arrive in the mail the next day."

Pravdin starts to protest but Friedemann T. waves his hand in his face. "No, no, no, no, no, I don't know what they're talking about, so for God's sake don't tell me." He turns to the empty street and calls out: "He didn't say anything, as God is my witness." To Pravdin: "For God's sake, give them what they want." Holding his overcoat on his agitated shoulders with trembling fingers, he hurries off down the middle of the street without another word.

"Yourself is whom you should have sexual intercourse with," Pravdin calls out to the retreating figure. He laughs nervously under his breath, surveys the walls for ears. "Onanism is an idea whose time has come," he yells, pauses for an echo that never returns. "Before you can have an advanced industrial society, you have to have a society." Pravdin does a silent jig under a street lamp, crosses over walking squarely on the pools of light, pushes through the heavy door into the lobby of the auditorium, presents his ticket to the usher guarding the entrance. "Don't tell me there is no Pravdin," he warns the usher when he appears to hesitate, "because you have the honor of having him before your very obsolete body."

The usher studies the ticket. "This is blue," he observes coolly. "Tonight is not blue. Tonight is green. Blue won't get you the time of day."

"The time of day is what I already have," Pravdin mutters, snapping the expanding bands of his watches for emphasis, "along with the month, the fiscal year and diurnal tides in the Philippine Sea."

Pravdin retreats into the street, scurries around the corner, turns into an alleyway, peeks in the stage door entrance of the auditorium. "Psssssssssst," he summons an old man sitting on a high stool, "have they started without me?"

"Oh, my, yes," the old man confirms the worst. "They've been at it for ten or fifteen minutes."

"I rush back like a madman from the short-hair symposium in Stockholm and they start without me," Pravdin complains bitterly. "Between us," he confides, flinging an arm over the old man's shoulder, "the vanguard of the proletariat has no respect for the rear guard of the proletariat is what the trouble is."

"I never mix in politics," the old man apologizes.

"Smart move," Pravdin tells him. He pads silently to the wings of the stage and regards the seven men and two women, each with a microphone planted on the table in front of them, who stare out at the eerily quiet audience. All nine fidget uncomfortably on straight-backed plastic chairs like chain-smokers in a no-smoking compartment.

"And so," the chairman of the Writers' Union, a stoop-shouldered short-story writer, is telling the audience, "we must acquire the possibility of differentiating between realism that is realistic, inasmuch as it portrays proletarian life in a positive fashion, and realism that is nonrealistic, inasmuch as it arbitrarily focuses on those portions of proletarian life which are atypical and thus portrays our society in a negative fashion." The chairman pauses to moisten his dry lips with a dry tongue, pulls the microphone closer to his face, continues; his voice is toneless; he reads from file cards without looking up at his audience. "What then is the role of the artist in a socialist society? The role of an artist in a socialist society is to act as a cultural fulcrum: to serve as a balancing point between the aspirations that originate from below and the directionality that originates from above. Under these conditions, any artist—"

The wind-up Don Quixote emerges from the wings, pivots mechanically toward a large floor electric fan that isn't running, changes its mind, rumbles under the table, lance extended, and starts down the line of legs. The two women sitting at the end nearest Pravdin scrape back their chairs in panic. One of the men ducks under the table, comes up with the Quixote tightly in his grip, passes it to the chairman, who waves it over his head and angrily cries, "Who is responsible for this? Who is responsible for this?"

"Cervantes, Miguel de," announces Pravdin, speaking into the microphone abandoned by the first woman panelist.

He turns toward the audience, is blinded by the spotlights that stab down at him from every side. "Comrade writers," Pravdin begins nervously. He swallows several times, reminds himself, *What we are here is literary.* "Comrade writers," he starts again in a stronger voice. "Proof positive, in the form of original manuscripts, is what I have to prove that Honored Artist of the Soviet Union Frolov is a plagiarist."

Pravdin squints into the spotlights, strains to catch some reaction from the audience: a shuffling of feet, gasps, coughs, anything. The chairman, the others on the platform, regard Pravdin coldly but make no move to interrupt him. "Comrade writers," Pravdin pleads, "it's this way: Before you appears a nobody to fill your ears with things you don't want to hear, to beg you to walk on water, move mountains, work up a sweat from a noneconomic activity. Here is the evidence"— Pravdin holds high the photocopies of the manuscript—"that a senior Soviet citizen has taken credit for something someone else wrote. So on one side, yours truly Robespierre Pravdin, a shrugless Quixote with unarmed truth. So on the other"—Pravdin gestures with his head toward the nine—"the vanguard of the vanguard, with their Maginot mentalities, holding the fort in crumbling cultural blockhouses."

Pravdin, unnerved by the utter silence that reverberates like a silent echo through the hall, takes a step backward, glances quickly toward the wings to make sure the stage door is still there. "What you can do is you can circumcise your hearts," he continues, "or you can pierce your inner ears so as not to hear what you don't want to hear. More to say I don't have. I thank you, very fine ladies and gentlemen."

The diaphragms on the spotlights close. Overhead, enormous crystal chandeliers glimmer dimly, brighten, flood the hall. Pravdin, pale as death in the white light, is suddenly chilled to the marrow of his brittle bones; he sees why there has been no reaction from the audience: a completely empty house is what he's been playing to.

"Aiiiiiiiii," he cries, sweaty and weak and unfortunately wide awake.

"You talk too much," sneers the chairman, packing away his filing cards.

"Waak, waak," barks Pravdin, "rev-lutions are verbose, rev-lutions are verbose."

CHAPTER 8

"How empty?"
demands Mother Russia . . .

"How empty?" demands Mother Russia. "Empty how?"

"Empty as in nobody there." Pravdin is snappy, irritated. He shivers, chilled by a wind not blowing, glances over his shoulder for the hundredth time.

"I wish to God you'd stop that," Zoya tells him. "It makes me nervous, and when I'm nervous I need to pass water all the time. If they want to follow us, let them for God's sake. Be like me. Ha! Nowadays when they open my letters they don't even bother sealing them professionally; they close them with transparent tape. But do I get all worked up? I shrug it off."

"I can't shrug," notes Pravdin.

"Shrug mentally," Zoya orders, "and stop looking back."

"I look back," Pravdin explains, "because I'm trying to turn them into pillars of salt."

"Very funny," says Zoya.

"Meant to be," says Pravdin.

Nadezhda tears off a page from her pad, passes it to Pravdin. "Couldn't you see it was empty?"

"All I saw were spotlights," he says wearily. "I assumed there were people there because I saw the chairman talking to them."

"What were his nails like?" Zoya wants to know.

"His nails were the last thing I would have noticed," Pravdin fires back.

"Don't jump on me," Zoya retorts.

"I'm not jumping," protests Pravdin.

"Apology accepted," says Zoya. "Dear Robespierre," she adds, linking her arm through his, "you were a dear man to even try. Here, this way"—she turns down a pathway between the rows of tombstones—"it's just over here." She stops before a worn stone with a legend eroded by time and lays a small bouquet of forget-me-nots on the mound of earth. "Here," she announces in a voice trembling with emotion, "repose the decaying bones of the poet Sergei Yesenin, who kissed me on the neck one wild, passionate night in 1925 and slashed his wrists in a moment of boredom the next. The funeral was incredible. Tears ran into the gutter in rivulets. Four women swooned. A sidewalk vendor made a fortune peddling smelling salts. From the limb of that tree a young woman named Galya hanged herself. I myself was inconsolable for two or three days."

Pravdin moves closer, makes out the dates on the headstone. "How come you put the flowers today when tomorrow is the anniversary of his death?" he asks.

"I prefer to commemorate the kiss," Zoya insists co-
quettishly.

Crossing a dirt field on the way back to the Metro stop,
Mother Russia asks Pravdin if he thinks she should let her
name be used in an ad in the United States of America by the
Singer Sewing Machine Company. Pravdin, absorbed in his
own thoughts, nods vaguely. "Who will be hurt?' 'he says.

"You really didn't hear a word I said, did you?"

Pravdin nods again. He is watching Nadezhda, who has
wandered off, is adjusting her telephoto lens, taking a series
of pictures of a peasant woman sitting on the back step of a
dilapidated apartment house picking with thick fingers
through a child's hair for lice. Pravdin finds a pointed stone,
scrawls in the earth:

Either the louse will defeat Socialism
or Socialism will conquer the louse

(V. Lenin: Pravdin has never been sure whose side he was on).

As Pravdin is about to descend into the subway, Mother
Russia asks: "What about the ad for Singer?"

Pravdin, looking over her shoulder, spots a short man in
a blue raincoat bending over in the dirt field and copying something into a notebook. "What ad?" he asks, preoccupied.

Pravdin gets off the train ahead of Mother Russia and Nadezhda, lingers for a time near the tomb of the unknown sol-
dier trying (without success) to sell Bolshoi tickets to visiting
Mongolians, makes his way at noon (bells sound the hours—
but miss by one) to the Hotel Minsk for a buffet luncheon
for comedians.

"Is Pravdin the name under which you perform?" inquires a young woman with too much lipstick and not enough
eye shadow.

"That's one way of phrasing it," acknowledges Pravdin.

The young woman moistens her lips, scans the invitation

list, finds a "Prastin" and a "Protenkin" with nothing sandwiched between them. She looks up, takes in his sneakers,
his trousers frayed at the cuffs, his Eisenhower jacket, his
day-old growth of rust-colored beard, his red hair going off in
all directions. "You don't look humorous," she concludes.

"Humorous is what I am," insists Pravdin. He folds himself into a comic crouch, winds himself up as if he is a Don
Quixote doll, starts his spiel. "Picture it: Roosevelt, Stalin,
Churchill at Yalta. Roosevelt takes out a solid silver cigarette
case, casually shows the inscription to the others. 'To F.D.R.,
from a grateful American people,' is what it says. Churchill,
not to outdone, produces a platinum cigar case studded with
semiprecious stones, casually shows the inscription to the
others. 'To the Right Honourable Winston Churchill, from
a grateful British people,' is what it says. Stalin comes up with
a spun-gold tobacco pouch studded with diamonds, emeralds,
rubies, casually shows the inscription to the others. It says, "To
Count Esterhazy, from the Vienna Yacht Club!' "

Pravdin freezes expectantly, but the young woman with
too much lipstick and not enough eye shadow doesn't crack a
smile.

"Not funny," she says.

"Waak, waak, not meant to be," retorts Pravdin. "How
about this one. Khrushchev delivers his speech to the Twentieth Party Congress denouncing Stalin, then takes his seat.
The vanguard of the proletariat responds with stunned silence. A note is passed up to the podium and handed to
Khrushchev. 'Where were you when all this happened?' is
what it says. Khrushchev turns purple with rage, charges like
a bull back to the microphone, waves the note furiously over
his head. 'Who wrote this?' he demands. Nobody moves a
muscle. 'That's where I was,' Khrushchev explains."

Pravdin freezes again but the young woman remains
stony faced. "Still not funny," she says.

"Waak, waak, still not meant to be," Pravdin replies, backtracking with a lopsided jig toward the street door.

Pravdin's stomach rumbles; he queues at a sidewalk stand, makes do with a stale *piroshki* and a warm glass of *kvass*. Picking at the pieces of *piroshki* stuck between his teeth with the nail of his little finger, he walks over to the pink prewar building in which the All-Russian Feminine Beauty Standards Bureau has its offices.

When his turn comes, Pravdin pulls from the bowels of his briefcase what appears to be a tube of cream.

"Someone's already invented toothpaste," says the tired functionary who nicked himself shaving and coagulated the blood with bits of toilet paper he forgot to remove.

"Toothpaste is what it's not," announces Pravdin. The functionary with the toilet paper on his chin assumes a judgmental posture in his chair, absently treats himself to spoonfuls of honey as he listens. "It's this way," Pravdin begins. "Depilatory cream is an idea whose time has come. Before you can build communism you must construct socialism. Before socialism, an advanced industrial society. And who"—the monologue is not particularly animated; Pravdin waves the tube about in the air out of force of habit—"ever heard of an advanced industrial society without depilatory cream!"

Pravdin hefts himself with an effort onto the desk. "Thesis: unwanted body hair. Antithesis: soft stubble-free skin. Synthesis—"

Pravdin's bloodless lips move, words form but no sound emerges; he is speechless with apathy. Exhausted, he sinks back into the chair. "Oy"—his palm slaps in anguish against his high forehead—"what is it I'm selling? And why?"

"Go on," encourages the functionary with the toilet paper on his chin. "This has possibilities."

"Synthesis," Pravdin mumbles, desperately trying to pick up the thread. His eyes, suddenly moist, close; a lid twitches.

"Synthesis: Ha! A wind-up Quixote emerging from the last wooden house in central Moscow to charge the holy of holies. Off my rocker is what I wish I was! *Der mentsh iz vos er iz, ober nit vos er iz geven.*"

"What language is that," the functionary asks in a kindly way, "Latin?"

"What it is is Jewish. It's an old Talmudic saying I just invented that means, 'A man is touch wood what he is, not what he was.'" Retreating toward the door, Pravdin produces from a pocket a huge handkerchief, mops his brow. "Hot is what it is in here," he complains, weak and wide awake—and sweating from a noneconomic activity.

Pravdin slips into the self-service elevator at the Hotel Rossiya with a group of women from the American Mid West. "Did you see the shoes," whispers one carrying a wooden babushka doll. "Their feet must be *pointed* to get in them."

"How about the trousers," ventures another, giggling. "If the legs were wider they'd be a skirt. Look at the trousers on this one!"

"Misses," Pravdin says with exaggerated politeness, "about the trousers, did you maybe notice how cuffs is what they all have. Cuffs"—he dances in place as if he has to urinate urgently—"are a covenant between the seventy-first incarnation of God, who is alive and well in the Sandunovsky Bath House, and *his* chosen people. Aiiiiiii," Pravdin cries, pressing his hand to his crotch in evident discomfort, "in is where I can't hold it any longer. Do you know, Misses, that in this worker's paradise we are not allowed to pee without a permit? I'm one of the privileged few who touch wood has one." He starts to unzip just as the elevator doors jerk open. The women gasp in relief, flee into the corridor. Pravdin, immediately calmer, continues on the fourteenth floor, makes his way to the barber shop, settles into a chair for a shave by a lady barber who has the habit of cradling her client's head on her abundant bosom. When the hot towels are covering all of Pravdin's face except his mouth, he turns slightly toward the man in the next chair, whose face is equally hidden, and asks in English:

"How did the Bolshoi interview go?"

"Pretty well," Hull replies in an undertone. "He came up with some great lines."

"Give me a for instance?"

"He said something about how the bosses have two choices," Hull says quietly, "they can convince us or kill us. Listen, something very strange took place at the Writers' Union Congress yesterday."

"Strange how?" Pravdin demands, his voice suddenly tense. "How strange?"

The lady barber removes the towels, strops the blade on a strip of leather, lathers Pravdin's beard.

"Think of me as hemophiliac," he instructs her through clenched lips as she clamps his head to her bosom.

"Talk less, listen more," she orders. With the back of her thumb she removes most of the lather, flicks it into a bowl, starts to shave him. For a while the only sound is Pravdin's labored breathing and stainless steel scraping against rough skin. When she finishes the lady barber wraps Pravdin's head again in hot towels.

"Strange how?" Pravdin repeats to the man next to him.

"Strange because nobody showed up except the union officers, who went ahead and made speeches to an empty house. According to what I heard, they were expecting somebody to turn up and make a plea. I'd be willing to pay through the nose to know who turned up, and what he said. How about it, Pravdin? Get a line on this for me and I'll really make it worth your while." When Hull realizes he is getting no response he peels the towels from his face, turns toward the next seat, discovers it is empty; Pravdin has already removed his feverish head from the barber shop.

Pravdin, clutching his stomach because of ulcers he's sure will one day come, makes his way down the fire staircase one flight to the twelfth floor (there is no thirteenth, there may be no Pravdin), hunts for the linen storage room where a woman he knows hides odds and ends left behind by tourists (combs, safety razors, hairpins, ballpoint pens, magazines, books, an occasional shirt or pair of suspenders, and so forth and so on) until he picks them up for resale. "Excuse me," Pravdin stops a chambermaid wheeling a cart full of dirty towels and used soap, "but room twelve-seventeen seems to have disappeared."

"There is no twelve-seventeen," snarls the chambermaid.

"And the linens, if it's not a state secret, are stored where," Pravdin leers at her, "in heaven?"

"There are no linens," the chambermaid hisses. "There is no heaven." She backs off a few paces, fills her lungs with air, starts pushing her wagon toward Pravdin as if she intends to run him down. "God is dead," she gasps. "Religion is the opiate of the people."

"Violence is what's the opiate of the people," Pravdin corrects her, sidestepping at the last instant, playing her past with his briefcase and a mumbled "Olé."

The chambermaid hurtles down the corridor, puts on her brakes, maneuvers her wagon around, starts back toward Pravdin. "Oy," he moans, "off her rocker is what she is." He scrambles into a stairwell, takes the steps two at a time, stops for breath at the eighth floor landing, scrawls with chalk on the wall:

They are capable of loving only the dead

(A. Pushkin: Pravdin speaks from long personal experience). He is drawn to a small rain-spotted window on the landing by the distant feedback of a loudspeaker system. Pravdin peers out, finds himself looking down on Red Square, which is filled with floats and ranks of sweat-suited gymnasts rehearsing for the May Day parade.

"Wave now, that's the way," a voice drifts up from the loudspeakers. "Remember to smile when you pass the reviewing stand. What is it? Not now, not now. You girls over there, don't just hold the flowers up, wave them. A little enthusiasm, if you please. That's better. Good, good. Where is the monitor? One, two, three, four and one, two, three, four and—No, no, the hoops go up on two and over the head on four. Those with fans, open on one, close on three. We'll begin from the beginning. Once again now. One, two, three, four and one, two, three, four and . . ."

Pravdin sinks back on his haunches, fingers his four overlapping medals, watches the marchers being put through their paces as if they were circus horses, watches one girl with long braids being instructed to spontaneously race up to the latest of the Great Mountaineers and thrust a bouquet of roses into his hands.

Slowly Pravdin drifts off into a daydream. In his mind's eye he sees himself waving to the huge crowd from the reviewing stand atop the holy of holies, which has been scented with vaginal deodorant spray for the occasion. The buildings on every side are draped in giant red cloths to keep the dust off during the spring cleaning. The cobblestones in Red Square have been scrubbed and waxed and covered with pages of *Pravda*. Animals Pravdin is afraid to identify prance by in lockstep pulling a float on which a half dozen actors are frozen into a statuelike tableau; it portrays the last Emir of Bukhara, Said Mirmuhammed Alimkhan, gazing serenely down from the Ark twenty meters above the city to watch the Friday executions. Below, the Druse, on his knees, is lifting his palms to the Emir for mercy as the executioner's knife slices into his jugular. "Aiiiiiiii," Pravdin cries as the float rumbles past on the copies of *Pravda*. He steps up to a microphone and cries out, "Waak, waak, Honored Artist of the Soviet Union Frolov is a plagiarist." Instantly his voice echoes from the speakers around the square. "Honored Artist . . . Honored Artist . . . Honored Artist . . ." A young girl detaches herself from the crowd, dashes up the steps to the reviewing stand, thrusts a bouquet with a note attached into Pravdin's hands. "What language is that, Jewish?" is what the note says. "Who wrote this?" Pravdin screams into the microphone, furiously waving the note over his head. ("Who wrote . . . who wrote . . . who wrote . . ." echoes from the loudspeakers.) When nobody steps forward, Pravdin flashes his crooked smile. "That's where I was," he says. "That's not touch wood where I am." ("There may be a Pravdin . . . there may be a Pravdin . . . there may be a Pravdin," echoes from the loudspeakers.)

Across from the Bolshoi, in the pale early evening shadow of a small fountain, an off-duty taxi driver with wild eyes is waltzing on gangling legs, head flung back, arms out, with a nonexistent partner. Suddenly he leaps to a stop before the gold-toothed woman who sells *kvass*, bows low inviting her to dance.

"How can you dance without no music?" she taunts him.

"But there is music," cried the off-duty taxi driver. "Can't you hear it?" He cocks his head, listens. "Crazed Misses Marmeladeev and her troupe of children dancing to her frying pan drum on the Voznessensky Bridge. Dostoyevsky heard it. I hear it."

The *kvass* lady shoves him away angrily. "Get off," she scolds, "and leave me be." The off-duty taxi driver laughs, waltzes silently off. A dozen or so hippies sitting on the edge of the fountain clap rhythmically.

"Comrade Eisenhower, hey ho, Comrade Eisenhower," calls Ophelia Long Legs as Pravdin lopes by heading for the Bolshoi. She catches up with him at the theater steps, tugs at his elbow. "Comrade Eisenhower," she tells him in an undertone, "the militia were nosing around this afternoon."

Pravdin stops short, draws Ophelia Long Legs into the lee of a column. "What did they ask?" he demands breathlessly.

"They didn't ask," she explains, "they looked. They posted a man at the front door so nobody could leave, then started at the attic and worked down. It's a wooden house and noises carry so we could hear them moving furniture and opening drawers. When they did Mother Russia's room, she sat in the kitchen drinking tea and composing letters out loud." Ophelia does a surprisingly good imitation. " 'To my adorable former classmate with the big ears and narrow nails, Leonid Ilyich Brezhnev, with copies to the *New York Times*, the London *Times*, *Le Monde*, the Voice of America, the Secretary General of the United Nations, the World Health Organization. Leonid Ilyich: your pimply ruffians in boring blue trenchcoats . . .' Oh, you should have heard her. The only time she lost her temper was when they told her one of her parrots had escaped out the window. He flew the coop when they opened the cage to search it."

"Which one?" Pravdin asks, on the alert for omens.

"The one that's always saying, 'Waak, waak, help, help.' "

"Vladimir Ilyich is who it was."

"Shhhhhhhh." Ophelia Long Legs looks around quickly. "Someone will hear you."

Pravdin laughs wickedly. "Picture it," he cries even more loudly, "Vladimir Ilyich splattering the holy of holies with white fungus and *waaking* away at the masses below. *Help, help, waak, waak.* Ha! What did the boys in blue do when they couldn't find anything?"

"How do you know they couldn't find anything?"

"Because the last wooden house in central Moscow is not where what they're looking for is!"

"So that's why they were so annoyed," Ophelia remembers. "When they left, the last one out angrily wrote something on a patch of dirt next to a tree. It probably was a code or something. It said, 'The louse will lose.' What does that mean, the louse will lose?"

"It's an old Talmudic saying," Pravdin explains, "that means, 'It's the bosses who'll watch the bosses.' "

"Who's Talmud?" Ophelia asks.

Pravdin only shakes his head, dips into his briefcase, comes up with a Beatles record that he offers to Ophelia.

"How much?" she asks suspiciously.

"A present is what it is," Pravdin says. Before she can not protest, he melts into the crowd hurrying up the steps to the Bolshoi for a performance of the ballet *Don Quixote.* At the third balcony he squeezes past four intense young women and takes his seat as the house lights dim. The giant curtain opens, the music swirls through Pravdin's head. His lids close. In his mind's eye he sees Frolov, a sturdy man in his seventies, sitting just where the unsigned note he found under his door said he would be: in the first row of the orchestra, his eyes glazed with lack of interest. The first act ends and he makes his way, along with several men and women tucked around his heels like bird dogs, toward the bar for a cognac his doctor has forbidden him to drink. Holding court in the bright light of the room where refreshments are sold, Frolov is suddenly confronted by a pale, fragilely thin man with wild red hair.

"Honored Artist of the Soviet Union Frolov?" the thin man demands.

Thinking he is being asked for an autograph, Frolov reaches for his fountain pen. The thin man with the wild red hair going off in all directions rears back and slaps the aging Nobel laureate across the face. *Thwak.* Everyone in the room is instantly and utterly silent. To Pravdin it looks like a *statue vivante* entitled "After the Slap." Even liquids seem to solidify in midair, in permanent pour between bottle and cup. Tears (of frustration, of anger, of pain, of fear even; who can say?) well in Frolov's eyes. Pravdin's voice rivets everyone:

"Honored Artist of the Soviet Union Frolov is a plagiarist."

The intensest of the intense young women taps Pravdin on the arm. His eyes open; the houselights have come on, the music has stopped. "I've never seen anyone watch a ballet with his eyes closed," she comments scornfully to her comrades.

"Attention," Pravdin cautions her in a stern voice, "those who are not with us are not with us." He climbs awkwardly over knees, makes his way down to the well-lit room where refreshments are sold. Frolov, a sturdy man in his seventies, is standing near the bar, his back toward Pravdin, sipping fruit juice. Pravdin, his pulse pounding in his temples, his eyes feverish, pushes through the crowd, causing one woman to spill wine on the dress of another.

"Honored Artist of the Soviet Union Frolov?" Pravdin addresses the man's back.

He turns, takes in Pravdin's basketball sneakers, his trousers frayed at the cuffs, his Eisenhower jacket with the four medals overlapping above the breast pocket, his red hair going off in all directions. "So it is you," he says.

"Honored Artist of the Soviet Union Frolov is a—"

Thwak.

Pravdin, his cheek stinging from the blow, reels back drunkenly. Tears (of frustration, of anger, of pain, of fear even; who can say?) well in his eyes. He looks around quickly; only half a dozen people nearest them have noticed anything out of the ordinary. Pravdin sinks into a comic crouch, cackles wildly, cries with all his force:

"Honored Artist of the Soviet Union Frolov is a son of a bitch."

His voice is lost in the din of conversation.

"The twentieth century," Pravdin yells, tears streaming down his cheeks, "is a time without an idea. Read the handwriting on the wall, Frolov is the louse who'll defeat Lenin. Better more but worse. Ha! I look sane but I talk crazy. To dine with the Druse use a long spoon."

Pravdin sees through his tears a blonde with a large wine stain on her dress bearing down on him. "You think you can bull your way through crowds and spill wine," she shrieks. Heads turn. Conversation stops. Liquids solidify in midair, in permanent pour between bottle and cup. "Look at this," the blonde cries tragically, holding high her stained skirt for everyone to see. Over her shoulder Pravdin catches sight of Frolov disappearing toward the exit.

"Gracious lady," he blurts, starting after him, but she bars his way, pushes him back.

"Who will pay for this," she demands, "is what I want to know?"

"Put salt on it," someone suggests.

"Ice water," a woman offers, "is the thing for wine."

"The juice of a lemon," advises a waiter, "is highly recommended."

"It's ones like you . . ." the blonde, distraught to the point of hysteria, begins to harangue Pravdin, jabbing her index finger into his solar plexus.

Pravdin retreats. "Talking stains is like talking about life after death," he murmurs. "I have thank you enough trouble with life before death."

The bell for the second act sounds. The crowd breaks up (reluctantly; Muscovites don't particularly like *Don Quix-*

ote). Folding himself into what is left of his dignity as if it is a tattered Army greatcoat, sweating from noneconomic activities, shivering from drafts from a window that isn't open, Pravdin hurries off toward the last wooden house in central Moscow.

They are waiting for him in the kitchen: Mother Russia and Nadezhda standing stiffly with their backs to the sink; Friedemann T., the beardless assistant rabbi and three other men sitting awkwardly around the table sipping out of politeness an infusion the aroma of which they can't support. There is, between them, an uncomfortable silence broken only by the delicate scraping of China cups on saucers and an occasional cough.

Pravdin takes in the scene from the door. "With me, one is unfortunately par, two is already a crowd, three has the makings of a conspiracy, but this"—he motions with his briefcase toward the reception committee—"a convention of the Supreme Soviet is what this looks like. To what do I owe the honor? Friedemann has come to talk about his new ballet based on Solzhenitsyn's *First Circle*, that much I can figure out. But the rest of you are expecting what from me? Swiss watches with wrist alarms? Carburetors for Fiats? Instant matzos even? Tickets maybe to Red Square for the May Day parade?"

One of the visitors, an intense young man with long curly sideburns and a heavy beard, angrily pushes away his cup, leaps to his feet. "I told you we shouldn't come," he blurts out.

"Calm yourself, Aaron," Friedemann T. tells him.

"Sit down," the assistant rabbi orders, pulling Aaron back into his seat. "There's still time to leave when he says no."

"No." Pravdin supplies the item so they can leave. "It

doesn't matter the question, no is my answer. So now is when you can all pick yourselves up and go home."

"Why so much belligerence?" the assistant rabbi demands. "Blood we're not asking for. Besides, how can you give an answer when you don't know the question? It's not biblical."

"Biblical times are what we don't live in," Pravdin explodes. "The chosen people is what we no longer are. Some big shot Old Testament prophet come to lead us in your frayed tallith and mended yarmulke to the promised land is what you're not!"

"For God's sake, Robespierre," Mother Russia cries, tapping the counter with her fly swatter in annoyance, "get hold of yourself. Listen to them. The one with the sideburns and beard has honest fingernails."

Pravdin turns on her. "If I'm worked up," he retorts, "I'm worked up over a noneconomic activity."

Nadezhda moves to his side, slips her hand into his, draws the back of his hand to her mouth and kisses it. Pravdin reddens at this very public gesture of affection, breathes deeply, calms down. "So what is it?" he inquires. "It must be life or death if you're drinking Zoya's infusions."

The five men put their heads together in the middle of the table and hold a quick conference. "You're at least a friend of his," Pravdin hears the assistant rabbi whisper. Silence. Finally Friedemann T. scrapes back his chair, faces Pravdin, adjusts his overcoat that hangs like a cape from his shoulders, clears his throat.

"What we are here is Jewish," Pravdin coaxes.

"Dear fellow, this is not a laughing matter," Friedemann T. chastises Pravdin. "It appears that the rabbi here, and Aaron, and myself, have been approached separately by representatives of the government and informed that twenty-five exit visas would be delivered to the Jewish Committee if a certain Robespierre Pravdin could be prevailed upon to return whatever it is they want him to return." Friedemann T. holds up a palm. "Once again I beg you not to say what it is they want. We don't know, and it goes without saying we don't want to know. Isn't that right, gentlemen?"

The others nod in agreement.

"In any case," Friedemann T. continues, "all of us here have a vested interest in this matter inasmuch as all of us have applied for exit visas. So we formed this delegation—"

Pravdin can't believe his ears. "*All* of you want exit visas?"

Friedemann T. squirms uncomfortably. "All of us, yes."

"Israel is where you want to go, Friedemann?"

"Israel and points west, yes," Friedemann T. acknowledges. He takes a step toward Pravdin. "You've got to do this for me, Robespierre. I'm sick of always being on the outside and trying to get in. I'm fifty-seven years old. *Fifty-seven!* I'm sick of gate-crashing. I want a standing invitation for my old age."

"Dear Robespierre," Zoya says, "give them what they want. Nobody can say you didn't walk on water."

"Three of the exit visas will go to you," the beardless assistant rabbi adds. "You can take anyone with you. Nowhere is it specified they have to be Jewish."

"You don't have the right to say no," Aaron says emotionally. "We have families, futures—"

"What makes you think there is a future?" Pravdin taunts him, taunts them all. "What makes you think we're not the point of time? Listen"—Pravdin sinks into a comic crouch, indicates with his eyes the walls have ears, continues in a stage whisper—"a while ago they offered one exit visa to get back what I have and they want. Today twenty-five. Tomorrow fifty maybe, a hundred even. All we have to do is hold out a month or two and we can get all the Jews out of Russia. All the goyim too; nowhere is it specified they have to be Jewish. Ha! Will the last goy to leave the country please close the lights! Picture it: a giant moving truck pulls up to the last wooden house in central Moscow and those funny men in blue raincoats start carrying in cartons of exit visas. Two hundred and thirty million of them. A mound—mound nothing, *mountain!*—of visas! We'll flood Israel with immigrants, they won't have room to turn around they'll be so many of them. A line of immigrants stretching from Odessa to Haifa walking on water to the Promised Land! And I'll be the one who did it. Robespierre Isayevich Pravdin, the man who got everyone out of Russia. Hero of Socialist Labor! The Order of the Red Star!! The Order of the Red Banner!!! The Order of Lenin even!!!! I'll maybe take Brezhnev with me. Also the big bosses of the Writers' Union. And all the bastards who turned down the Q-Tip. Listen, rabbi, you want to do something for the Jews? Stay in Russia and mind the store when we all leave."

"You have no heart," the beardless assistant rabbi laments.

"A heart is what I have," Pravdin corrects him. "Wounded is what I thought it was, but it turns out, touch wood, to be only circumcised."

CHAPTER 9

Pravdin sleeps
on his side . . .

Pravdin sleeps on his side, his back to Nadezhda, his arms hugging his torso as if he is in a straitjacket instead of pajamas. Snatches of song drift through his head. At times he remembers the words, not the music; at times the music, not the words. He struggles to join the two together as if they were halves of a broken saucer, but the glue (squeezed from a tube of depilatory cream) doesn't hold. Frustrated, he tosses onto his back, is suddenly pricked into consciousness by an omen: an old man in the alley outside the house is sharpening knives on a pedal-driven wheel and calling out, in a singsong voice that has both the words and music, "Knives, scissors, blades of all manufacture, honed until they bleed."

Pravdin shuffles to the window, looks out over the eucalyptus branch on the sill to watch the peddler at his work. Feet pumping, he bends over his wheel and presses with three fingers of his left hand the blade against the grindstone. Soft silent sparks angle off in all directions: a miniature fireworks from the collision of molecular worlds maybe. Civilizations too small to be imagined, destroyed in the blink of the peddler's goggled eye! Straining, Pravdin can almost make out a distant "Aiiiiiiii." He shivers uncontrollably from tiny catastrophes, inaudible whimpers. Nadezhda comes up behind him, throws a shawl over his bony shoulders, draws him back toward the bed.

They make love in the dancing shafts of sunlight that slip through the leaves outside Nadezhda's window. "Knives, scissors, blades of all manufacture," the peddler's chant reaches them from the cul-de-sac. Pravdin struggles to get his mind off worlds disintegrating without so much as a decibel count. "Honed until they bleed." Nadezhda becomes aware of his softness, senses his lack of concentration, takes corrective action. Soon the bed springs and floorboards are drowning out the inaudible whimpers in Pravdin's skull. Their bodies press together like halves of a broken saucer and off he comes—not an instant too soon.

Later, Nadezhda passes him a page from her notebook on which she has written: "You tossed during the night. Did you dream?"

"I dreamed I was trying to reconstruct a dream I wasn't sure I ever had," Pravdin replies sleepily. "Bits and pieces were all I got."

"Give me a bit, give me a piece," Nadezhda writes.

"There was something painfully bright, a searchlight maybe, stabbing toward me from far away," he remembers. "It hurt my eyes so I squinted into the dream, which had the physical form of a tunnel, to cut the glare. As soon as I did that I could make out the scene: I was vacationing in a gigantic hotel on the Black Sea reserved for KGB interrogators. God knows how I got there, but there is where I got. They assumed I was one of them and started to ask me about my score, my techniques, my favorite cases. Criminal is what we are here, I told myself, so I gave them ten minutes of police bla-bla-bla. Something I said made them suspicious— probably the item about how I tortured suspects by scenting their cells with vaginal deodorant spray. Next thing, they had me strapped to an animal I was afraid to identify and something painfully bright like a searchlight was stabbing toward me from very far away. It hurt my eyes so I squinted into the dream, which had the physical form of a tunnel, to cut the glare. And so forth and so on."

"Your dreams are like cylinders on a player piano," Nadezhda writes. "The same thing keeps coming around again."

"Also my life," Pravdin mutters.

Nadezhda passes him a note she has obviously written the night before. "Zoya wants you to return the original manuscripts and so do I. Don't argue, Robespierre. Neither of us realized how stubborn you were when we got you into this. I remember your story about making sandals from watchstraps, but I didn't believe it. I do now. You will give it up, won't you? We can make a life together, the three of us—me, you, Zoya. We don't need to set things straight. Life is too short."

"Maybe yes, maybe no," Pravdin tells her, but she can see from his expression that she has made some headway.

"Maybe yes, maybe no," Pravdin repeats to Mother Russia over a breakfast of rice-cake cereal and steaming glasses of tea sweetened with spoonfuls of jam.

"Maybe yes, maybe no," Zoya scolds, wagging a wrinkled finger under his nose. "Your life is one big maybe yes, maybe no. You've done everything you could. What, for God's sake, did you hope to accomplish by slugging Frolov in front of everyone at the Bolshoi?"

"I thought they would have to arrest me and the truth would come out at the trial," Pravdin explains lamely.

Zoya is almost hysterical. "Trial! Who said anything about a trial! Where is it written you have to go down with the ship?"

"A little idealism," Pravdin mimics her, "is good for the digestion, heartburn, headaches, neuritis, neuralgia and sexual potency."

"Idealism is an ideal," Zoya fires back, "not a formula for everyday survival." She softens, touches his arm. "Dear Robespierre, you have been a real hero in a nonheroic epoch. You have lived up to the promise of your fingernails. But there's no use beating your head against a wall." She gestures with her fly swatter to indicate that the walls have ears. "Tell them where you hid the originals and it will be the end of it. Go ahead, tell the walls where the manuscripts are."

"*Power to the powerful, power to the powerful, waak, waak,*" comes from the partly open door of Mother Russia's room.

Pravdin laughs wickedly, turns toward the wall, opens his mouth to speak, shuts it as Ophelia Long Legs bursts into the kitchen gasping for breath from having taken the steps two at a time. "The militia which came yesterday—"

"Calm down, child," Zoya orders. "You'd think it was the end of the world."

"At the end of the world," Pravdin quips, "go to America—everything happens fifty years earlier there."

Ophelia takes three or four deep breaths, starts again. "The militia came back and left this in the postbox. It's for Comrade Eisenhower. Here." She holds out the brown envelope to Pravdin.

He takes it, opens the flap with a kitchen knife, reads,

rereads, passes it without a word to Mother Russia. Nadezhda reads it over her shoulder. "What does this mean?" demands Zoya.

"What this means," Pravdin explains coldly, directing his words toward the wall, "is that I am obliged to move out of Moscow within seven days. My residence permit is what the bosses have canceled."

"What is this 'administrative surveillance'?" asks Zoya.

"Is Comrade Eisenhower in trouble or something?" Ophelia looks from one to the other.

"Administrative surveillance," Pravdin tells Zoya, "means that sunset is what I can't go out after, public places I can't put my head into, more than one person at a time I can't speak to, daily is when I have to report to the KGB."

Nadezhda scribbles furiously, hands a note to Mother Russia. "He can trade them—the residence permit for the manuscripts!"

"Of course he can," Zoya seizes the idea eagerly. "This is a negotiating situation."

Pravdin flings his words at the wall. "*Der mentsh iz vos er iz, ober nit vos er iz geven.*"

"What language is that, American?" Ophelia Long Legs asks.

"What it is is Esperanto," Pravdin declares. "It's an old Talmudic saying I just rediscovered that means, 'I know what it is I'm selling. And why.' "

Pravdin buttons his Eisenhower jacket, tightens the laces on his sneakers, starts down the staircase, which creaks agreeably under his feet. *Count your blessings,* he reassures himself. *You're reasonably healthy, you know what you're selling and why, and you live in the last wooden house in central Moscow. Touch wood.* (His bony knuckles rap on the polished banister.)

He runs into Master Embalmer of the Soviet Union Makusky on the front steps. "Are you still tending the Great Leader, the Living Light?" Pravdin's nostrils flare; the odor of formaldehyde is unmistakable. "Ha! I smell the answer! Attention! The cult of the personality is antisocialist and out of place in a country that prides itself on progress. One step back, no steps forward. The revolution *is* capable of regretting."

Master Embalmer Makusky chews on his cuticles, not sure what to make of Pravdin's outburst. "Those who are not with us—" he begins.

Pravdin finishes the sentence for him. "—will be stashed away in some holy of holies."

Pigeons scatter. Emaciated squirrels claw their way up trees. An old man sunning himself on a bench angrily waves his cap, but Pravdin, out of earshot, hurtles on across Sokolniki Park oblivious to the small signs seeded around that say:

Comrades: the grass belongs to you, so
KEEP OFF

At Khokhlovka, a district of factories and warehouses, Pravdin can just make out scrawled in faded chalk across a billboard:

Nothing worth knowing can be taught.

He reaches for his chalk, substitutes "preached" for "teached," adds underneath:

Fear and the pit and the snare are upon thee,
O inhabitant of the earth

(Isaiah: Deutero-Pravdin wonders which Isaiah was the real Isaiah?) Pravdin, chilled to his bones by a cold front that hasn't yet reached Moscow, makes his way to the Druse's warehouse.

Zosima opens the small rear door before he has a chance to ring.

"Marx-Engels-Lenin-Organizers-of-Revolution is whom I want to see."

"There is no Melor," says Zosima. "He is a figment of your imagination."

"The Druse then," Pravdin insists. "Is Chuvash also a figment?"

"Chuvash has been summoned," she explains, avoiding his eye the way one avoids looking at a condemned man, "to the city of Ashkhabad."

"What is he selling?" Pravdin sneers. "And why?"

"Services," Zosima replies as if the answer is as plain as the comfortingly long lifeline on Pravdin's enormous palm. "To open again to the faithful the door of mercy, to conquer Mecca and Jerusalem, to convince the world of the inevitability of the Faith, to demand obedience to the seven commands of Hamza, the first and greatest of which requires truth in words—"

"And so forth and so on," groans Pravdin. The door clicks shut in his face and he is left staring into a peephole in which he has been reduced to the only occupant of a teardrop world.

At every intersection uniformed militiamen and auxiliaries with red armbands give Pravdin a casual once-over, but it isn't until he is within sight of the Kremlin walls that he comes across a serious control point.

"Papers," barks a beefy major.

Pravdin produces from a hip pocket his internal passport. The major scrutinizes it meticulously, compares with narrowed eyes the photograph against the original standing, appropriately deferential, before him, studies with suspicion the signature, glances at the word "Jew" penned in alongside entry three, takes in Pravdin's Eisenhower jacket, his basket-

ball sneakers. Expressionless, the major snaps shut the passport, hands it back, indicates with a toss of his head that
Pravdin is to continue on his way.

"Mother Russia is certified," Pravdin berates himself under his breath as he hurries off, "but I'm the one who is out
of his mind."

"Were you addressing me, comrade?" the major calls
after him.

"I was mulling over some lines from one of Lenin's articles," Pravdin explains. "You know the one; it's called, 'I
know what is to be done.' "

Automobile traffic thins, pedestrian traffic swells: dele-
gations from factories, collective farms, schools, hospitals,
drift toward Gorky Street to take their places on line for the
great pass-in-review that will last seven hours. There is a good
deal of tension in the air, an electrical charge that follows
a thunderstorm. Police whistles hoot nervously, uniformed
arms gesture excitedly, the flow is directed between freshly
repainted yellow lines. Three men in black suits struggle with
an enormous wreath across which is strung a banner that
reads: "Lenin is the light." Little girls with pigtails scamper
around their heels, squealing at a game of tag. Half a dozen
young men in blue sweatsuits trot by carrying aloft a poster
that says, "Vladivostok Institute for Applied Science" and
another that proclaims: "All Power to the Soviets."

"Papers," orders a crew-cut man with fat thighs in a
tight civilian suit at the entrance to Red Square.

"Pravdin, Robespierre Isayevich," Pravdin announces,
holding out his internal passport, "at your beck and call." He
silently clicks the heels of his sneakers, half bows. "I am
invited to the reviewing stand set aside for Heroes of the
Soviet Union," he explains, pointing to one of the four
medals dangling on the breast of his Eisenhower jacket.

Beyond the civilian, just inside the entrance to the square, the brass Army band strikes up the "Internationale" as it sets off in lockstep toward the reviewing stand. Instantly hats are whisked off heads, knees stiffen, chins jut forward, eyes glaze over, minds wander.

"Entrance during May Day," the crew-cut civilian shouts over the music, "is by written pass only."

Pravdin promptly flashes a laminated card, mumbles something about representing the Second Chief Directorate of GLUBFLOT. The civilian catches his wrist in an iron grip before he can put the card away, draws it closer for a better look.

"This is a menu from an ice-cream parlor," he snaps. His eyes narrow; his voice takes on an ominous tone. "What did you say your name was?"

In the square the "Internationale" ends. Throaty cheers rise like balloons and hang for a moment over the cobblestones. A gleaming convertible with a pot-bellied marshal of the Army anchored erect in the back makes its way down an endless line of soldiers. From behind Lenin's Tomb a thousand white pigeons soar with an audible flutter of wings into the still sky.

The parade, Pravdin senses, is off to a reasonable start. Touch wood.

"Pravdin, Robespierre Isayevich," Pravdin supplies his name in a shaky voice. He leans toward the crew-cut civilian, presses two Bolshoi tickets into his palm. "I have friends in high places," he pleads. "I could use influence, but I don't take advantage of my name . . ."

"Pravdin," the civilian repeats, pocketing the tickets, running a finger down a list looking for the P's. His finger suddenly stops, taps the list twice. The crew-cut civilian looks up in surprise. "There is a Pravdin," he says. He shouts a command to two soldiers, who advance toward Pravdin. He starts to back away on trembling legs.

"Honored Artist of the—" Pravdin calls out.

"Get him," hisses the civilian. "There is a Pravdin."

"Soviet Union—" Pravdin is yelling now at the top of his lungs, is yelling and backtracking and ducking under a barrier and scampering toward the holy of holies, the two soldiers hard on his heels, the civilian too. Soldiers converge on him from all sides.

"Frolov is a son of a bitch plagiarist," Pravdin screams just as he is tackled from behind, is pounced on by three more soldiers, by half a dozen civilians, is pinned and smothered under blue raincoats and straitjacketed by men who are experienced in such matters.

"Aiiiiiiii," Pravdin rants, "ridiculous is what we are here. So who needs to walk on water. So cotton doesn't begin with Q. So who was hurt? Unarmed truth is a disaster for the digestion, heartburn, headaches, neuritis—"

A gag is drawn over Pravdin's mouth. He struggles to speak, sinks back onto the cobblestones. Tears (of frustration, of anger, of fear even; who can say?) stream down his cheeks. A stain spreads along the inside of his thigh.

"What's happening?" a woman on the fringe of the crowd demands excitedly. "What's going on?"

"Only a gate-crasher," her companion explains.

Perched on a flagpole overhead, well out of arm's reach, a green-crested parrot observes with a beady eye the collision of molecular worlds, hears Pravdin's inaudible whimpers, croaks:

"*Waak, waak, help, help.*"

CHAPTER 10

Crusts of snow . . .

Crusts of snow cling to the hard ground like moss. Dead branches slant through at ridiculous angles. The sloping terrain in between is dotted with thin ink-black puddles, many of them covered by a wrinkled, watery film of ice. Beads of frozen dew glisten in the honed air. Pravdin, pale as death (hustlers, like Hasidim, avoid the sun), wearing a frayed quilted jacket with a faded number stenciled on the back, trudges up hill parallel to the ski lift scavenging for odds and ends lost in the snow during the season. The sack tied to his belt jingles with loose change, false teeth, steel-rimmed eyeglasses, rings, wristwatches, also a ceramic eye. Something attracts his attention over to his right. A medal gleams in a patch of sooty snow. Then another. Four altogether. Hero of Socialist Labor! The Order of the Red Star!! The Order of the Red Banner!!! The Order of Lenin even!!!! Pravdin polishes them on his sleeve, pins them on the breast of his quilted jacket, continues up the slope toward the tree line. He comes across a woman's compact, a gold fountain pen, a ring of rusted keys, an identity bracelet with the name "Stasa" etched on it, a brooch with a likeness of Stalin inside. Pravdin shivers, starts back down, stumbles over the bleached skeleton of an animal he is afraid to identify, begins to run, sinks to the cold ground gasping for breath next to a sign that says:

Comrades: the snow belongs to you, so

KEEP OFF

In the distance an old man with a Roman nose and a Lenin-like beard angrily waves a ski pole tipped with cotton, but Pravdin hurtles on into the safety of a forest, stops short in terror when he sees the trees are made up of their component parts.

"Aiiiiiiiii," screams Pravdin, sitting upright in bed, sweaty and weak and wide awake. A small observation panel on the bolted door slides open. "Pee is what I have to do," Pravdin yells at the eye he knows is there.

"You don't have a permit to urinate at night," a muffled voice replies.

"How do you know it's night?" Pravdin argues weakly. A cheek muscle twitches. His eyes water. "You're lying. Day is what it is and day is what I know it is." He falls back onto the pillowless cot. The four whitewashed windowless walls, sulfurish in the yellowish light behind the steel grille that stays lit all the time, appear to tilt on their axes. "Turn out the light at least," Pravdin begs. "I can't sleep and I can't not sleep." The observation panel slams closed; the sound reverberates in Pravdin's skull. "The worst thing was the slamming of door," he remembers Mother Russia saying. He tosses to one side, then the other, stares at the hands on the wall electric clock, which are moving in a counterclockwise direction, giving Pravdin the sensation of going back in time. "The future may be futureless," he moans, "but there may be a past, there may be a Pravdin." He relives the interrogation in the KGB complex on Dzerzhinsky Square, remembers staring for what seemed like an eternity at the unbroken red wax seal on the office safe, recreates Melor's voice repeating over and over, "Article one ninety dash one of the Soviet legal code makes it a crime to disseminate falsehoods derogatory to the Soviet state and social system."

"Where is the crime?" Pravdin demanded the first time they went over the ground, "disseminating falsehoods that happen by coincidence to be derogatory to the system, or derogating the system with information that happens by coincidence to be false?"

"You don't understand," Melor explained patiently. "If it is false, it follows that it is derogatory."

"What about disseminating truehoods that also happen to be derogatory?" Pravdin probed for weak spots in Melor's logic. There were none.

"Something that is true cannot at the same time be derogatory."

"Ha!" retorted Pravdin, "I have you. That Frolov is a plagiarist is a truehood. That powerful bosses protect him from the consequences of this truehood is derogatory to the system."

"Because you say Frolov is a plagiarist doesn't make him a plagiarist," Melor countered.

"Proof is what I have," Pravdin muttered, tiring of the game.

"Produce it," challenged Melor, and he added: "I'm

talking about originals, not photocopies, it goes without saying."

"Without saying," Pravdin agreed, "is how it goes."

The minute hand on the counterclockwise clock makes its noisy way from eleven to ten to nine. Pravdin continues back in time, relives the trip in the ambulance to the KGB complex, the straitjacketing on the cobblestones of Red Square, the slap at the Bolshoi, the speech to the eerily quiet Writers' Congress, the interview with the Poet, the appointment with the prosecutor, Nadezhda's birthday party, and so forth and so on. He winds up, half asleep, squinting into the sulfurish light that remains lit all the time, scavenging for odds and ends in the snow after his release from the camps. He is pinning on the four medals when the door to his room opens and Half-Again Dimitri, the largest of his three warders, enters with a tray, which he deposits on the edge of the only piece of furniture in the room, the bed.

Pravdin squirms into a sitting position. "In is where I can't hold it any longer," he begs Half-Again Dimitri. "A permit for daytime peeing is what I have."

The warder plays with the lobe of a cauliflower ear, looks at his watch, shakes his wrist to get it going again. "It's supposed to be self-winding," he says to himself.

"Self-winding is what we're all supposed to be," Pravdin moans, clutches his crotch in agony.

"I suppose it will be all right," Half-Again Dimitri says, and he indicates with a toss of his head that Pravdin is permitted to follow him. Half-Again Dimitri steps into the long white corridor, taps on the metal door three times with a large key. At the far end of the corridor another guard taps back three times, the signal that no "clients" (as the guards call the inmates) are coming or going; in this wing it will go badly for the warders if clients so much as catch sight of one another. Pravdin, toilet trained, slips his feet into his laceless basketball sneakers, grips his pajamas by the waist to keep them from falling around his ankles ("No laces includes no belts," the guardian instructed him when he arrived—only God knows how long ago!), follows Half-Again Dimitri down the corridor, hugging the wall opposite the clocks, all of which are running—but at varying speeds, and in different directions. (At the check-in, Pravdin stole a look at the date, figured out that the place was being run on the Julian calendar, thirteen days behind the Gregorian twentieth century.) The W.C. is the only one Pravdin has ever seen without graffiti over the urinal. His bladder bursting, he closes his eyes, luxuriates in the act of peeing, imagines he is writing with urine in the snow:

Violence is the opiate of the people

(G. Mendeleyev: Pravdin wonders if anyone will see the penis-writing in the snow), shuffles back to his room to attack the meal that Half-Again Dimitri has deposited on the bed.

Nothing is what works out the way you expect, Pravdin consoles himself. Campwise from his twelve years on location, he assumed he would learn the ropes in a matter of days, install himself in some advantageous position (straitjacket custodian maybe, or trustee in charge of night peeing), institute the official exchange rate (four fistfuls of bread equal to one bowl of soup equal to eight grams of tobacco equal to enough cloth to wind three times around an average foot), settle into a routine that would have as its ultimate goal the painless passing of time. But how can time pass painlessly when he is no longer sure in what direction it is moving? And at what rate?

Everything conceivable has been done to disorient the clients. There are no windows in the building through which light, or night, can pass, or at least Pravdin has never come across any in his escorted wanderings around the corridor to the W.C., to the (daily? semiweekly? who can say?) therapy sessions, once to the infirmary for an enema lovingly administered by a male nurse with sour breath. It is impossible to keep track of the time of day from the dozens of electric clocks, because each one has a different story to tell. The meals are no tip-off either: after what Pravdin takes to be a sleepless night, Half-Again Dimitri will turn up with a lunch, followed a couple of hours later by a breakfast, followed eighteen hours later by a second breakfast. It is enough to drive a man off his rocker.

For a while Pravdin thought he had figured out a way to beat the system. It worked this way: Pravdin, as far back as he could remember, always emptied his bowels around nine in the morning. Now a trained sphincter muscle, he reasoned, couldn't be thrown off by the absence of windows, or clocks that ran counterclockwise, or random meals. For what Pravdin took to be two weeks, his sphincter worked like a clock. But someone must have figured out his system, because the next thing he knew he was forced to drink some bitter liquid that constipated him for what he took to be several days (or weeks; who can say?), a state of affairs that ended with the loving enema from the male nurse with sour breath.

Pravdin's last resort was his beard. From God knows what obscure reach of his jackpot mentality he summoned up the fact that beards grow more quickly during the night, so he spent endless hours (or an entire day; who can say?) fingering the stubble on his chin what he took to be every few minutes. He must have been spotted through the observation panel, because Half-Again Dimitri stopped turning up with an electric razor to shave Pravdin. His rust-colored beard is long enough now so that he can just catch sight of the tip if he strains his eyes in the bottoms of their sockets.

It goes without saying that there are no mirrors. No mirrors includes no unpainted metal surfaces, no place where enough water can collect to give back a reflection. (Even the toilet bowl is dry.) Well, reflections he can do without, but the thing that makes Pravdin's skin crawl is the total absence of wood. No wood means no reassuring incantations about being reasonably healthy, relatively sane and a resident in the last wooden house in central Moscow.

"How are you getting on?" inquires the interrogator, whose name is Doctor Berezin, when Pravdin is brought to his office for another therapy session. "Anything you'd like to complain about?"

Clutching his pajamas, Pravdin puts on a bold front. "Other than no water in the toilet bowl, no regular bowel movements, no shaving, no windows, no wood, no conversations with other clients, no regular meals, no idea what time of day it is, what day of the week it is, what week of the month it is, what month of the year it is, there's nothing particular I'd complain about, no," Pravdin says. But he can't sustain it. Coiling into a comic crouch, he whines: "My right arm is what I'd give for a line on diurnal tides in the Philippine Sea."

"Very revealing," comments Doctor Berezin, a heavy-lidded latent intellectual whose eye movements lag a fraction of a second behind his head movements, so that the act of looking is made to seem like an afterthought. He wears a white laboratory coat with a plastic flower in the buttonhole and tobacco stains on the lapels.

"Not meant to be," mutters Pravdin, taking his usual place on the plastic seat in front of the plastic desk.

Doctor Berezin studies for a long time his handwritten notes in Pravdin's dossier.

"We left off"—the doctor's head, then his eyes, come up from the dossier—"with my suggestion that your attempts to slander Honored Artist of the Soviet Union Frolov were

motivated in part by your unconscious desire to win the respect of Nadezhda Oos, with whom you are in love. Have
you had a chance to think more about this?"

"Thinking is what I don't do much of," Pravdin explains
with a cackle. "I spend most of my time trying to calculate
what time it is. If you would tell me, other things are what I
could occupy myself with."

"Think about it now," the doctor instructs Pravdin.
"What do you see as your motive?"

"About why I was doing what I was doing, I never
thought much," Pravdin insists. "Frolov is a fake. I assumed
all I had to do was show the right person the evidence and
that would be the end of him."

"Don't you see that you are obsessed with changing the
system?" Doctor Berezin says, and he adds: "Your type always
thinks you will change things. You will have the impact of a
footprint on water."

Pravdin shakes his head gloomily. "Beating the system is
what I'm obsessed with, not changing it."

"I suggest that your obsession has at its roots the twelve
years you spent in the camps during the period of the cult of
the personality." Doctor Berezin massages his lips with the
eraser at the end of his plastic pencil. "I suggest that you
harbor paranoid delusions about reforming society. But have
you ever stopped to consider that a completely fair society, in
which no citizen could blame circumstances beyond his control for his failures, would be a disaster? The idea astonishes
you, I see. Yes, a disaster. Instead of being able to shrug off
failures as the inevitable result of social unfairness, we would
have to attribute them to our own shortcomings. Resent-
ments would build up and eventually rip apart the social
fabric. Don't you see that a certain amount of arbitrary unfairness is essential to any advanced industrial society?"

"I can't shrug off failures because I can't shrug," Pravdin says moodily.

Doctor Berezin is annoyed by the response. "Is that all you have to say?" he demands sharply.

Pravdin presses his palms over his ears. "I have invented a new genre," he groans, "the genre of silence."

The doctor is impressed with the phrase, copies it into the dossier. "Who said that?" he asks, looking up with his head, then with his eyes.

"I said that," Pravdin retorts.

Pravdin, back in his room, finds a breakfast tray waiting for him on the edge of his bed. He passes up the cold toast, drinks the lukewarm tea from the plastic cup. His palm slaps against his high forehead: *Plastic cup! Why didn't I think of that?* He casually turns his back on the observation panel in the door, snaps off the plastic handle, grinds down the scar by rubbing it against the stone wall. After a while Half-Again Dimitri removes the tray without comment. Pravdin, his spirits soaring, fingers his treasure. He sits on the floor and begins to tap on the wall, using an old Siberian prison code that substitutes numbers for letters.

"Hello to anyone," he taps quietly on the wall.

There is no response.

"Hello to anyone," he taps more urgently.

There is a faint tapping from the other side. Pravdin counts quickly, decodes hungrily this first contact with another client. "What time is it?" is what the neighbor wants to know.

"No idea," Pravdin taps back. "How long you been in?"

Before the answer arrives Half-Again Dimitri appears at the door, signals with his key to make sure the corridor is free of clients, leads Pravdin back to the interrogator.

"We left off," Doctor Berezin murmurs soothingly, "with you claiming you had invented a new genre, the"—he consults his notes—"genre of silence is what you called it."

"That was just a few minutes ago," exclaims Pravdin in agitation.

The doctor is surprised. "That was yesterday," he coldly corrects him.

"Oy," Pravdin buries his head in his hands. "I could have sworn it was a few minutes ago."

"Why do you cringe like that?" asks the doctor. "Are you afraid of me?"

"I must be," Pravdin answers. "Otherwise why am I making such an effort to like you."

"I'm not sure I follow?"

"Against people we're afraid of," explains Pravdin, "our only defense is to like them so that they will like you back for liking them. In the camps every prisoner knew that it was the first sign of giving in to fear when he began to like his jailers. I must be afraid of Half-Again Dimitri too, because yesterday (or was it last week; who can say?) I found myself thinking he had a sympathetic face."

"There is no reason why you shouldn't like me," Doctor Berezin offers. "I am, after all, on your side, though it may be difficult for you to see this clearly right now. The official who is dealing with your case considers that you are guilty of ideological sabotage, but I am of the opinion that your actions are a symptom of a curable mental condition."

"You're off your rocker," Pravdin says, "if you think I'm off my rocker."

Doctor Berezin is not offended. "Only a trained psychiatrist can detect mental illness in its formative stages. Most of our clients are unaware of their condition. Even members of their families, or close friends, don't notice anything, or misinterpret what they do notice. At first everyone protests, out afterwards many of our clients and their relatives come back to the hospital to thank us." The doctor smiles. "Perhaps you will return to thank us too one day."

Doctor Berezin pushes a plastic button on his desk. Almost immediately Half-Again Dimitri turns up at the door to escort Pravdin back to his cell, where he finds another breakfast waiting for him on his bed. "Breakfast I just ate," whines Pravdin.

"That was yesterday," says Half-Again Dimitri.

As soon as he is alone Pravdin taps on his neighbor's wall with his treasured bit of plastic. "How long ago did I leave off tapping?" he asks.

"An hour," the answer comes back, "or maybe a day. Who can say?"

"How long you been in?" Pravdin repeats his question.

"Months I think, but it may be a year, I'm not sure. How about you?"

"Two weeks is how long I was here according to my sphincter muscle," Pravdin taps quietly, "but they constipated me and then gave me an enema. Now I only shit water so I don't know how long ago the two weeks ended."

"What are you in for?" Pravdin's companion wants to know.

"Gate-crashing," he taps back. "How about you?"

"I climbed out on a limb," the neighbor replies, "for a crazy man who came to me with a story that Honored Artist Frolov is a plagiarist. I believed him and started to investigate the case."

Pravdin is sick to his stomach. "Oy," he moans, presssing his palms with their long lifelines over his ears. "More is what I don't want to hear."

Days (or weeks; who can say?) pass. Doctor Berezin keeps coming back, in the therapy sessions, to the question of motive. "If we could dig deeply enough into your motivation," he explains, "I think you would see the light of day and return the original manuscripts."

"Maybe yes, maybe no," Pravdin comments tiredly; he has been kept up all night (or all day; who can say?) by the tapping on his wall, to which he didn't have the heart to respond.

"Make an effort," the doctor encourages him.

Pravdin, bored by the doctor's persistence, decides to give him a dose of political bla-bla-bla. "What I was doing," he says, "was testing whether there really is a difference between communism and capitalism, or whether they merely disagree over who owns the means of production, a relatively unimportant detail since what is important today is not who owns the means of production but who controls it." Pravdin sees that Doctor Berezin is scribbling away in the dossier, waits patiently until the doctor's head, then his eyes, come up. "As I understand it," Pravdin goes on, "capitalism relies on the essential corruptibility of the individual; that is the foundation on which it is constructed. Communism, on the other hand, is based on the belief in the essential incorruptibility of the individual when confronted with the truth. So I confronted certain individuals with a certain truth." When the doctor looks up again, Pravdin adds: "One poor silly bastard listened, the rest ran."

"Let's pass over motive for a while," the doctor suggests, "in favor of more traditional avenues of investigation. Let's talk about the animal that keeps turning up in your dreams, the one you are afraid to identify. Do you have an idea what it is?"

Pravdin shakes his head.

"A dog or a cat perhaps?" Doctor Berezin prompts. "A horse or a camel?"

Pravdin shakes his head again.

"What about the baby carriage? You remember"—the doctor checks the dossier—"eyeglasses shattered, the baby carriage hurtled down the steps, you were obsessed by who is in the carriage. In a subsequent dream you found out, but you refused to tell me. Perhaps you will confide in me now. Who was in the carriage?"

Pravdin studies the ceiling for a long while. "The animal I'm afraid to identify is who was in the carriage," he says finally.

"Ah, now we're getting someplace." The doctor seems grateful for the information. A gleam comes into Pravdin's eye as he watches him scribble excitedly in the dossier: if acting sane got him into this joint, then it follows that acting insane will get him out! His palm slaps his high forehead. *Why didn't I think of this before: insanity is an idea whose time has come.* "Something else is what I should tell you," Pravdin stage whispers, leaning forward eagerly. He rolls his eyes, mutters something about the walls having eyes, ears, a nose, a throat, sexual problems even, lowers his voice so that Doctor Berezin has to strain to hear him. "I come from the future. Ha! The idea astonishes you, I can see. Yes, yes, the future is where I come from. I'm working my way back through all my incarnations to my original incarnation." Pravdin is on his feet now, leaning across the desk. "At each incarnation along the way, I try to disrupt events so that they create a future that doesn't contain me, so I won't exist to travel back in time."

Doctor Berezin stares at Pravdin in a new light. "Why would you want to do that?" he inquires.

Pravdin practically climbs across the desk in excitement. "Because I've seen the future and it needs work," he exclaims triumphantly. He clutches his temples to contain the hot flashes of panic. "I was *Homo Economicus* about the time of Cro-Magnon," he says, flexing his primitively long thumb as if it is irrefutable proof. Suddenly Pravdin leaps clear of the desk, grimaces crookedly, backpedals with a little jig toward the door. "Don't you hear it?" he demands, cackling wildly, gasping for breath, "the music of the spheres is what it is: crazed Misses Marmeladeev and her troupe of children dancing to her frying pan drum on the Voznessensky Bridge. I hear it. Aiiiiiiiiiiii."

A bearded Jew of indeterminate age leans against the sulfurish wall, his eyes sealed, his high forehead pressed to the imprint of a crucifix. Shots ring out, a ragged volley first, then a single shot from a smooth bored naval pistol. Pravdin starts, opens his eyes, sees for the first time the imprint of the crucifix. A horrified expression crawls across his face like a crab. At that instant a key turns in the lock, the door swings open with a squeal.

"Who is it?" he demands.

Who it is he'll never know because he is startled by an insistent tapping on the wall—not the one on the public prosecutor's side, but the opposite wall. Pravdin counts the taps, decodes. "Greetings," is what the client on the other side is sending over and over.

Pravdin answers reluctantly. "I'm trying to sleep," he taps out with the plastic handle of the cup.

"What are we here?" the client in the next room wants to know.

"Oy," Pravdin moans, sick to his stomach again. He taps back: "What we are here is crazy."

Half-Again Dimitri passes Pravdin his tray at the door. For days (or weeks, or months; who can say?) he hasn't stepped inside because of the handwriting, in feces, on the wall. Directly facing the door, in large sculptured letters, Pravdin has written:

I've seen the future and it needs work
(L. Steffens: Pravdin weeps every time he reads it).
On the public prosecutor's wall he has written:
Hustling will make you free.
On Friedemann T.'s side he has written, over his pillow-less cot:
Mist, bell sounds and brokenness.

When Half-Again Dimitri returns to collect the tray, he collects Pravdin too. "Something out of the ordinary for you today," he explains, signals with the key to make sure the corridor is client-free, leads Pravdin in a direction he has never been before, pausing at each twist in the hallway to get the all clear for the stretch ahead.

Beyond one right angle bend in the corridor they come across the sheet-draped body of a man lying on a rolling metal table. "I thought another client is whom I wasn't allowed to see," Pravdin comments sarcastically.

His sarcasm goes over Half-Again Dimitri's head. "The regulations cover only live clients," he says. He gestures with his large key toward the dead man. "Suicide. Cut his wrists with the plastic handle of a cup, which he sharpened on the wall." Before Pravdin can protest, he whips off the sheet so that he can see the corpse.

Pravdin gasps, doubles over and throws up on his lace-less sneakers. When he straightens again his lower jaw is twitching uncontrollably. He stares through moist eyes at the naked body of the young prosecutor: the skin appears to be drained of blood; white gauze has been wound tightly around his left wrist; lumps of sugar have been placed on his eyelids to keep them from opening.

"Dear God," Pravdin moans, sways, starts to tap his head against the wall in sequences of three. Half-Again Dimitri restrains him from damaging state property (the wall? the head?). Pravdin rants softly. "We are the chosen people, as evidence whereof we have cuffs on our trousers. I'm a big shot Old Testament prophet come to lead us in my beltless pajamas and laceless basketball sneakers to the land where you can pee without a permit."

"Calm yourself," Half-Again Dimitri implores.

"A windowless holy of holies is what we're in," cries Pravdin. White-jacketed guards come running from either end of the corridor. Pravdin squirms free of Half-Again Dimitri's grip, sinks into a comic crouch that is totally devoid of humor, screams over and over:

"Yahweh, Yahweh, Yahweh, Yahweh, Yahweh, Yahweh."

Pravdin is given an injection, calmed, carted off to a white amphitheater where he is strapped into a plastic swivel chair. He is blinded by spotlights that stab down at him from every side, squints into them, strains to catch some reaction from the audience: a shuffling of feet, gasps, coughs, anything. The diaphragms on the spotlights close. Overhead, lights buried in the ceiling glimmer dimly, brighten, flood the amphitheater. Pravdin, pale as death in the white light, is suddenly chilled to the marrow of his brittle bones; he thinks he sees in the half-circle of balconies that overlook the small stage familiar faces: the bulky lad with the sack of empties who scolded him for defacing a public notice; the one-eyed war veteran from the public prosecutor's office; the policeman who caught him jaywalking; the expressionless lady at the housing agency who pocketed his Bolshoi tickets; the street vendor with the wind-up Don Quixotes; the tired man with thinning hair and his pregnant wife who were moving out of the flat in Dzerzhinsky; Zosima; Ophelia Long Legs; Porfiry Yakolev, the weatherman with the handlebar mustache; Master Embalmer Makusky, biting away on his cuticles; General Shuvkin, with his left sleeve neatly pinned back to the shoulder; the second prosecutor, who fractured his tibia skiing in Zakopane; the Poet, deep in conversation with his housekeeper; A. N. Kulakova, the lady doctor who analyzed the Q-Tip; the thin bank manager who rejected the sperm bank; the man with the toupee who turned down the vaginal deodorant spray; the functionary with toilet paper coagulating his shaving nicks; the lady barber with the enormous breasts; the chambermaid who tried to run him down in the hall; also the beardless assistant rabbi; the blonde at the Bolshoi who accused him of spilling wine on her dress even.

Sedated, feeling as if he is walking on water vapor, Pravdin watches through a haze as Doctor Berezin outlines his case to the full house. "Antisocialist onanism," he is saying, "was the first concrete indication of the patient's essential alienation from the established order; a symptom, if you will, of the disassociation of his personality that was to become more profound as time went on. Scavenging in the snow shortly after his release from the camps, he came across four medals. According to his own account he immediately pinned them on and created a war-hero personality to go with them. From his earliest days he was attracted to fantastic schemes that had no roots in reality. In the camps, for instance, he spent two and a half years trying to produce a shoe from confiscated leather wristwatch straps. More recently he has pursued with paranoid preoccupation such diverse world-saving schemes as instant matzos and vaginal deodorant sprays."

"And cotton toothpicks," A. N. Kulakova shouts down from the balcony.

"Sperm banks too," adds the thin bank manager.

"Don't forget the slanderous attacks on Honored Artist of the Soviet Union Frolov," calls the Poet's housekeeper.

Pravdin concentrates on opening his eyes, or closing them, he's not sure which.

"This disassociation from reality morbidly embedded in

his personality," Doctor Berezin continues, "was really an early manifestation of incipient schizophrenia. The split in his personality can be clearly seen in the fact that he wore two wristwatches, one set to Greenwich Mean Time, the other to Moscow time, and both of which register diurnal tides in the Philippine Sea. Yes, diurnal tides! The idea astonishes you, I can see. But what could be more pertinent? Isn't this the subconscious showing to the world its quintessential dualism, hence the *di* or *two?* It is as if the separate personalities of Pravdin are washed by separate tides."

Suddenly Pravdin is drowned in a Greek-chorus of accusations:

"Obsessed with sex . . . three times in one night," cries Porfiry Yakolev.

"Split personality . . . Robespierre Pravdin vs. Comrade Eisenhower," shouts Ophelia Long Legs.

"Suffers from monomania . . . psychotic fixation on one world-saving scheme," accuses the man with the toupee.

"Neglect of personal appearance . . . frayed cuffs . . . basketball sneakers . . . seldom shaves . . . general apathy . . . emotional insensitivity," complains the chambermaid who tried to run him down.

"Hallucinations . . . delusions . . . convinced he alone has access to the truth . . . that he is being persecuted because of this," declares the second prosecutor.

"Exaggerated sense of his own importance . . . thinks at various times he is a famous author . . . well-known physicist . . . professional comedian . . . master chess player," calls the expressionless lady who pocketed his Bolshoi tickets.

"Incipient schizoheterodoxy . . . accompanied by paranoid delusions of reforming society," asserts the Poet.

"Overestimation of his own personality . . . poor adaptation to the realities of the social environment . . . thinks he's

an Old Testament prophet," wails the beardless assistant
rabbi.

"Uncontrollable emotions . . . bathetic . . . heightened
nervousness whenever he deviates from the norm," scolds the
street vendor of wind-up Don Quixotes.

"Morbid fixation with death after life," ventures Master
Embalmer Makusky.

"Liar," taunts General Shuvkin. "There were no campaigns."

The one-eyed war veteran from the prosecutor's office
leans over the railing. "In my opinion," he declares sadly,
"he's off his rocker!"

Pravdin buries his chin on his chest in shame. A pajama
sleeve is rolled up; a needle punctures his skin. "Aiiiiiiiii," he
cries, sweaty and weak but not sure whether he is wide awake
or sinking into the soft center of a nightmare.

A blind woman swabs with a Q-Tip the empty socket of an
eye; a man whose fingers have been chewed down to the
knuckles treats the cavity in the crotch of the Great Leader,
the Living Light, with vaginal deodorant spray; a boy with a
grotesquely long thumb reaches into a deep hole to feed
matzos to dozens of wriggling vipers. Pravdin, drugged,
drifting, clings to the broken images as if they were buoys,
but the male nurse with the sour breath descends on his erection with chapped lips, draws it slowly into his mouth, strokes
it with a tongue as roughly caressing as a cat's. Pravdin lets
the images slip through his fingers, moans, opens his swollen
lids, cries out in agony when he realizes that it may not be a
dream. With a panicky effort he tries to pull free, feels himself coming off—too soon, too soon. The male nurse accepts
his flow, smirkingly sucks the last drops from him as Pravdin
drifts off again into a region where images bob like buoys in

ink-black puddles covered with wrinkled, watery films of ice.

"He's burning with fever."

The words come from far away. Pravdin searches end-lessly for a position in the bed that doesn't hurt; the least movement has become painful. The lack of movement too.

"Spasmodic loss of muscular control."

Doors slam like smooth bore pistol shots. The smell of sulfur clogs his nostrils.

"Skin rashes."

Fingers take his pulse. A face leans close to his; he senses it hovering.

"WHERE . . . ARE . . . THE . . . MANUSCRIPTS? THE . . . MANUSCRIPTS . . . WHERE . . . ARE . . . THEY?"

Eyeglasses shatter; the baby carriage hurtles down the steps.

"Excessive saliva. Depression. Brain damage is a risk we can live with. He must be made to talk. Another dose of sulfazin."

A wind-up Quixote wheels on its horse and jerkily charges, lance level, a cardboard windmill; a needle punc-tures Pravdin's arm. Images burst.

"WHERE . . . ARE . . . THE . . . MANUSCRIPTS? WHERE . . . ARE . . . THE . . ."

Pravdin slinks back into consciousness, sulking in its shadows for days (or weeks; who can say?) before he emerges, breech-born, into a world of polished metal surfaces, toilets with water in them, also mirrors. "Oy," he groans, slowly runs the tips of his fingers across the welts on his upper arm. Sunlight slants across the bed. Pravdin blinks back a rush of emotion. Dear God in heaven, a window! Daytime! Time! Greenwich Mean Time even! Two wristwatches tick away on a night table next to his bed. Achingly, he twists his neck, luxuriates in the second, the minute, the hour, the month, the fiscal year. Also the diurnal tides in the Philippine Sea! His Adam's apple bobs. *My cup,* he tells himself, *runneth over.*

Someone across the room clears his throat. Pravdin painfully props himself up on an elbow, sees that he has a roommate; there is another patient in the metal bed against the other wall studying him with dark mistrustful eyes.

"Abalakin, Maksut Mustarkovich," the man introduces himself. He is big boned, with shiny stainless steel teeth and red welts on the bridge of his nose from steel-rimmed spectacles.

"Pravdin, Robespierre Isayevich," Pravdin responds weakly. "What are you in for?"

"They say I'm mad," the new neighbor explains. He massages the bridge of his nose with his thumb and forefinger.

"So," Pravdin asks, "are you?"

"I'm not sure." Abalakin hesitates, says finally: "The truth of the matter is I come from the past."

"Ha!" exclaims Pravdin. "I come from the future. What better place for the future and the past to meet than in this holy of holies!"

Abalakin laughs uneasily. "I really do, come from the past I mean."

Pravdin sinks back onto his pillow. A pillow! After a while he swings his feet over the edge of the bed, slips them into his sneakers, ties the laces. Laces even! "How can you pee around here?" inquires Pravdin.

"You take yourself down to the second door on your right in the hallway, you open your fly . . ."

"What about permits?"

"Permits to pee?" Abalakin asks.

Pravdin is incredulous. "Anytime you want is when you can pee?"

His roommate nods, regards Pravdin as if he is off his rocker. Pravdin takes himself down to the second door on his right in the hallway, opens his fly, pees into a toilet bowl with *water* in it, luxuriates in the sound of water spilling into water, glances at himself in the mirror over the sink when he washes his hands, turns quickly away when he sees someone he doesn't recognize. He is thinner, paler, bloodless almost, it seems to him; his cheeks are sunken, his eyes lost in the shadowy depths of hollows.

"What's the lowdown on the building?" Pravdin inquires when he returns to his room.

Abalakin has drawn up a chair in front of the open window and is sitting on it stark naked, sunning his hairy chest. "It's a sane crowd, generally speaking," he says, making no effort to conceal his bitterness. "On the side nearest the W.C. is a stress engineer who wrote a letter to the United Nations complaining about the lack of Soviet assistance to the struggle against imperialism in Vietnam. His roommate is an astronomer who published a report on black holes; it turns out that black holes are antisocialist. This same astronomer once discovered a comet and it was named after him. It recently whizzed past the earth a mere three hundred thousand light-years away. We celebrated the occasion by shaking up a bottle of water until it was bubbly and toasting his sanity. Let's see, on our side we have a genuine Jewish activist who started a hunger strike to the death when they refused him an exit visa on the grounds he was involved in secret work; he was a cutter in a factory that made military uniforms. He's being fed intravenously because strikes of any kind are antisocialist, you see. His roommate is a car mechanic who was caught running a black market operation on spare parts; spare parts are also antisocialist. The car mechanic passes the time, believe it or not, reciting all four conjugations of some Latin verb in the twenty-four tenses of the active indicative, passive indicative, active subjunctive, passive subjunctive, plus the four participles, the five infinitives, the five declensions with their six cases, and all the other clutter of that wretched language. Latin is anti—"

"Socialist," Pravdin finishes the refrain for him. "So you speak Latin?"

"I did," Abalakin says mysteriously.

"How about Yiddish?" Pravdin asks.

"I was Jewish once," Abalakin says, "Sephardic Jewish, not Ashkenazi Jewish. I spoke Ladino. Would it be asking too much to ask you if you're going to pass gas, would you do it in the hallway. Day or night. I'll do the same for you."

Pravdin likes Abalakin well enough but he has the feeling that the other man is avoiding him. After several days of peeing noisily into the bowl whenever he feels the remotest pressure on his bladder, passing gas in the hallway, watching with a great sense of well-being the seconds, minutes, hours, tides tick by on his watches, Pravdin puts it to Abalakin: "Bad breath is what I don't have," he insists. "So what is there about me not to like?"

Abalakin is spit-shining the steel rim of his eyeglasses, the steel caps on his teeth. "Over the years I have been obliged to spend a great deal of time in asylums," he explains. "It is my experience that half the clients in them work for the police, and the other half would if they were invited to."

"An informer is what you think I am!" Pravdin howls.

"Put it this way," Abalakin says, "if I don't tell you anything, there's nothing you can pass on to the doctors whether you are or aren't."

Pravdin sulks in his corner of the room without saying a word to Abalakin. Mealtimes come and go in silence. A lady librarian passes with a cart full of books; Pravdin borrows a copy of *Ten Days That Shook the World*, discovers the last page of each chapter has been torn out, goes racing after her to exchange, has to be restrained by white-coated guards when she refuses on the grounds that house rules limit him to one book a week. Two days go by in silence.

"What's not right?" Abalakin finally inquires in a tone that indicates he is ready to let bygones be bygones. Pravdin doesn't respond, instead writes on the wall over his bed:

Those who are not with us are us

(R. Pravdin: Pravdin has come a long way from the days when he was neither for, neither against, as God was his witness), spends the rest of the afternoon, part of the next morning illuminating (with colored pencils supplied by the lady librarian) the first letter of each word.

"Listen, Robespierre Pravdin," Abalakin finally appeals to him. "I made a mistake and I admit it. I'm apologizing." He offers his hand.

Pravdin, never one to hold a grudge, accepts it instantly.

"What's this about you coming from the future?" Abalakin wants to know.

"That"—Pravdin rolls his eyes to indicate the walls have ears, lowers his voice—"was a story I made up to make them think I was off my rocker. I thought they would let me go if they were convinced I was insane." Pravdin laughs nervously. "Ha! At least I thought I was making it up. Now I'm not so sure. What about you coming from the past?"

"That's real," Abalakin says intently. "I know you'll think I'm crazy. Everyone thinks I'm crazy when I tell them. I remember fourteen distinct incarnations before this one." His face takes on a swollen look; his eyes stare trancelike into Pravdin's pupil as if he is looking through a tiny hole into another universe. "Once I was wounded at the siege of Khiva in the Kara Kum desert. An old woman with no hair sucked the pus from my wound. I must have told her about other incarnations because I was thrown into a pit full of crazy people next to the guard house. I died there of plague. Once

I voyaged to Persia with the train of the one they called Tamer the Lame. We crossed great deserts, guided from oasis to oasis by the fires in the turrets of the minarets. I got drunk on wine in Persia and spoke of my incarnations and was put in another asylum, where I died quickly of a pain in the stomach that the doctors were unable to diagnose. I think now it was appendicitis."

"I always wound up in an asylum when they found out about my incarnations. Nobody believed me. I'm going to finish this life in an asylum too. I'm a walking compendium on lunatic asylums; physical conditions have improved in the last thousand years, though things are about the same with respect to the intelligence of the doctors." Abalakin grabs the lapel of Pravdin's pajamas, pulls him close. "Once I fought against Napoleon. I lost all my toes to frostbite and spoke of my incarnations when I was feverish. When I got well they put me in an asylum for army veterans near Moscow. I met a nobleman there who had been cheated out of his patrimony by a half brother who claimed the nobleman wasn't legitimate, then had him committed. The nobleman knew where there were documents proving his parentage, but they wouldn't let him out to get them. So he rotted in the asylum. He believed me when I described my incarnations and told me where the documents were so I could set things straight in my next incarnation."

"And did you," Pravdin wants to know, "set things straight?"

"As soon as I was old enough to write, I wrote an anonymous letter to his heirs telling them where the documents were. They filed suit and won the case. Once I was a boss," he continues, drugged by his own story. "I was the last Emir of Bukhara, Said Mirmuhammed Alimkhan. I held the power of life and death over my subjects. People kissed the hem of my robe."

"You lived in the Ark twenty meters above the level of the city?" Pravdin asks incredulously. "You were beardless and spoke with a stutter?"

"How do you know these things?" Abalakin demands.

"Every Friday you made your way, in finely worked golden slippers, along the carpets laid between the Ark and the mosque."

"Yes, yes. Later, I would return to the Ark through the twin towers, climb the steps between the prison cells to the balcony to watch the executions."

"Do you remember someone who lifted a palm to you for mercy?"

"They all lifted their palms to me for mercy, but I never granted it," Abalakin whispers. "How do you know these things?"

"There was one who asked for mercy who had the triangle of a seer on his palm."

Abalakin slumps weakly to the floor; Pravdin's lapel slips through his fingers. "There was one who had the triangle of a seer on his palm," he acknowledges. "I had the hand cut off at the wrist and brought to me."

Pravdin turns away. "Dear God," he murmurs, "you're telling the truth!"

Incarnations flicker before Pravdin's eyes like frames from an old Eisenstein. Eyeglasses shatter; the baby carriage hurtles down the steps, picks up speed, travels back in space and time to Bukhara. Pravdin grips the side of the carriage and peers over the edge, feels the wind in his face, sees far below Chuvash Al-hakim bi'amrillahi lift a palm with the triangle of a seer on it to the Boss of Bukhara, Maksut Mustarkovich Abalakin, who smiles down in a kindly way as the executioner's knife cuts through the Druse's jugular. "Aiiiiiii," cries Pravdin, sweaty and weak and wide awake. He sits up in the darkness. *Chances are he's insane, in which case no harm will be done. Dear God, look what I've been reduced to! But what if he's not insane? If he's not, he can write an anonymous letter in his next incarnation, tell where the manuscripts are, set things straight.* Pravdin remembers Mother Russia's story about Lenin saying what do we have to lose and shuffling off to the toilet before the Bolshevik revolution. *Me too, what do I have to lose?* Pravdin thinks.

In the inky blackness of the night, he gently shakes Abalakin awake, whispers for several minutes in his ear. Abalakin nods, gratefully squeezes Pravdin's shoulder. He is very moved, he whispers, by this proof that Pravdin believes him.

Pravdin crawls between the sheets of his bed, sinks immediately into a deep and dreamless sleep. When he wakes in the morning Abalakin is gone, along with his bedding and his few personal possessions.

In midmorning Pravdin's Eisenhower jacket and trousers are returned to him. They have been dry-cleaned and pressed. Shortly after lunch he is summoned to a front office and handed a paper bag containing four medals, a box of Q-Tips, a can of vaginal deodorant spray, a tube of depilatory cream and asked to sign a receipt. Pravdin, nostalgic for the ordered sweetness of shtetl life he never experienced, feels faint, puts a hand on the wall to steady himself. "Is something not right?" the matron asks in a concerned voice. Pravdin's bloodless lips move, words form but no sound emerges: he is speechless with humiliation.

Half an hour later he is given a certificate of insanity and released from the asylum.

Zingers to Singer:

The letters of
MOTHER RUSSIA

My very dear and obviously delightful Mister Singer,
Copies to: Soviet Ministry of Trade, Import Section
        United States of America Ministry of Trade,
        Export Section
        United States of America Embassy, Moscow

I had the misfortune several years ago to come into the pos-
session of your adorable little automatic stitching machine,
model number SW106. I say misfortune because although it
makes sewing easier it takes something (I'm not sure what)

away we had before we sewed on a Singer. But that's another story. Very shortly, come to think of it, almost immediately after I acquired my Singer it started tearing the fabric when it was supposed to be stitching it which was a catastrophe as opposed to an annoyance because in those days though not so much any more fabric, especially French or Italian, was difficult if not impossible to come by and once come by treated as a treasure. So you will I hope understand that the tearing of the fabric was something I tried to stop immediately with zero results since there was nobody I could find who would admit to being familiar with a United States of America machine even though it was a pre cold, even pre world war model. Nobody that is until one night last year at of all places a wonderful mainly Bach concert I met a sewing machine repairman with honest if dirty fingernails who let slip he had worked on Singers before the war and batting my still sexy eyelashes I talked him into taking a peek at mine which is how I finally discovered that what I need is:

Shuttle race

Why I am writing you if you haven't divined it already is in the expectation that you will supply to me the service après vente mentioned in your manual as your point forte (my instruction booklet is in French) for which I am taking the liberty of thanking you in advance.

Yours most appreciatively,

Volkova, Z. A.

Post Scriptum: I have been criticized for the hopelessness with which I distribute parentheses which (aren't they?) the building blocks of stream of consciousness, so I hereby offer you a handful which you can sprinkle on to taste.

(((((((((((((((((((((((((((())))))))))))))))))))))))))))

25 March

My very dear (and presumably delightful) Mister Singer,
Copies to: Soviet Ministry of Trade, Import Section
        United States of America Ministry of Trade,
        Export Section
        United States of America Embassy, Moscow
        Soviet Foreign Ministry
        United States of America Foreign Ministry

Ha! Good question. In my naiveté I assumed I could simply present my aging though still angular body at the door of the United States of America Embassy here and give to one of those prissily correct gray-suited assistant something-or-others rubles which he could then convert through some obscure bookkeeping process into dollars which could then be passed on to you. Well we all have (isn't it so?) our illusions. My favorite to which I am forever faithful is that there is a logic or more precisely an order to the world when all of our senses five shout at us that the world or the little we know of it suffers from an essential lack of harmony, an ugly dissonance, a seductive vulgarity, almost as if the music of the spheres were a concerto for vacuum cleaner and orchestra with an occasional solo (do you at all see what I mean?) by one of your darling Singers. Enormous stretches of time and space conspire to rob life of its harmony and (as one thing leads more often than not to another) its meaning and dignity. I have a feeling which is threatening to become a theory that we must make great efforts to find dignity and meaning and let's not forget harmony in the details of daily life, which is why I suggested in my first zinger dear Mister Singer that your darling little stitching machine takes something away from us in return for permitting us to sew more rapidly. Here you must surely be asking yourself, then why on earth does she want to repair hers? to which I can only respond I am hooked on speed and have been ever since my father relented and took us for an excursion in his new horseless carriage at a time which now seems so very very long ago. But back to the crux which is (isn't it?) how am I to pay you for the Shuttle Race? The precious young lady who shares the top floor of the next to last (and if what I hear is true, soon to be last) wooden house in central Moscow suggests that we barter. Do you recognize the word? I have already identified what I want from you so now you must identify what you want from me. My young lady friend has an idea you might like to have some old photographs of our Russian battlefields strewn with corpses but I told her that I suspected (correct me if I'm wrong) that you Americans are only interested in the dead when they are individually wrapped. Here we still cry at holocausts. But that's another story. In any case I am quite prepared to barter with you or if you can figure out how payment can be arranged to pay you, as the price of four dollars and seventy-five cents plus mailing seems to me to be ridiculously reasonable. I am obliged to tell you that Volkova, Z.A. is a Misses and not a Dear Sir, which point I am emphasizing by adding to my signature the more or less nickname that certain white-coated führers have bestowed upon me. Trusting to hear from you I remain as always someone who understands the hopelessness of life, yet hopes she is wrong.

Volkova, Z. A.
Mother Russia

Post Scriptum: How is it (I am curious, even eager, to know) that one can write a letter to a Mister Singer and receive a response to this very same letter from a Mister Prolnor? Naughty, naughty Mister Prolnor who ever you are, didn't your mother teach you not to read other people's mail? Here it is done all the time bien entendu. In the bad old days they used to take a certain pride in their work and reseal the letters professionally and it was hard to know if they had (as we suspected) been opened, but nowadays the bureaucratic rats who are responsible for incoming mail are rushed for time or lazy or amateurish or all of the above because they simply seal them up again with transparent tape. Still Mister Prolnor one expects more from the United States of America after all the advertising you've done about freedom of expression and that sort of thing. So I remain hopeful that my zingers to my dear and presumably delightful Mister Singer will elicit a response from the man of that very name.

                                               12 April
My dear (and to give you the benefit of the doubt, original) Mister Singer:
Copies to: Soviet Ministry of Trade, Import Section
          United States of America Ministry of Trade,
          Export Section
          United States of America Embassy, Moscow
          Soviet Foreign Ministry
          United States of America Foreign Ministry
          Chief Editor, The New York Times
          Chief Editor, Pravda

I am extremely touched (even, I'll say it openly, teary) at your offer to waive payment of the four dollars and seventy-five cents not to mention mailing, but I would very much appreciate an additional burst of information on what kind of waiver it is you want me to sign and what exactly your advertisement about a satisfied client behind the Iron Curtain would say, because (and here is the sticking point) I'm not at

*all sure you will want to represent me as saying what I really
think, which is that Singer ruined sewing.* You surely understand (then again considering your moral isolation perhaps you
don't) that being published in any way shape or manner in the
West is a sensitive (to say the least) affair here and even yours
truly who has been certified has been grilled for what appeared between the lines when one of my zingers to little
Leonid Ilyich turned up in your adorable New York Times.
Do Americans read too between the lines? The funny thing
about my letter appearing in the New York Times was that I
never sent it to the New York Times. But that's another
story. I did send it to some (you'll excuse the expression)
newspapers here but they filed it where they file all my letters, which is under P for poubelle. This (I'll admit it) in-
furiates me, though if I had a grain of sense I'd pull my
foxes more tightly around the very neck once kissed by (do
you recognize the name?) S. Yesenin the night before he
slashed his milk-white wrist, and take comfort from the company I keep. Face it, Dostoyevsky was also not published and
today isn't all published. Dear passionate Yesenin was considered (before he slashed his beautiful wrist) a counter revolutionary and God knows what after. Mayakovsky was written
off as a political hooligan. It required twenty or thirty years
for us to get back our lovely Bunin and dear cryptic Bulgakov
and beloved (though not by everyone) Platonov. Mendelstam
and Voloshin and Gumilev and Klyuev and Zamyatin and
Remizov will (God willing) be returned to us some day, but if
they must wait for publication so should I, except when it
comes right down to it wait is what I can't, which is why I
keep shooting off my zingers as if they were tracer bullets. As
for the import license, I really have no idea how one goes
about getting such a thing since generally speaking that kind
of operation requires a working (if that's the word I'm looking
for) knowledge of the bureaucracy which I, unfortunately (or

maybe fortunately) have so far avoided. But all is not by any means lost. There is a new roomer in our attic with pale nails who looks as if he knows his way around, and I will see if he can help. He has an interesting face too, an unholy combination of worldliness and naiveté, almost a kind of sane zaniness. Something happens to a person's face after the age of twenty for which he is (don't you agree?) responsible. But that's another story. The (new as we have taken to calling him) attic has big plans of his own to develop a kind of cotton-tipped toothpick designed to replace the key as the principal ear cleaner. The reason I pass this tidbit on to you is that if the Q-Tip (as he calls it) isn't already licensed in the United States of America you will want to look into it. I can't agree by the way with you when you suggest that the world has no existence except in terms of the objects we perceive in it because if what you say is (which I don't for an instant believe) true, nothing would have an existence except in its being perceived and the world (it follows, doesn't it?) would dissolve into an anarchy of individual perceptions. But from my point of view, which is to say from the second floor of the now last wooden house in central Moscow (since the next to last is being torn down), there is a curious order that runs through our perceptions, almost (and here I sense you shuddering) as if there is an underlying order to the universe, which takes me right back to the illusion I spoke about in my previous letter. Anxious to hear from you, I remain someone who regrets that time isn't a straight line but rather a circle or more properly a cycle made up of anniversaries and birthdays and occasions manqué which keep rolling around again to tease us with what might have been.

Mother Russia

Post Scriptum: It is reassuring, even (dare I say it?) comforting, to be once again in direct contact with the Mister Singer to whom I originally wrote. I do hope you weren't too hard on dear Mister Prolnor for intercepting your letters. Do send my best, bordering on cordial, greetings to him whoever and wherever he is. I wonder if it would be imposing upon your fabled generosity to ask you in your next letter (assuming there is a next letter), to describe in great detail inasmuch as it fascinates me, your fingernails.

20 April

My dear (though I'm beginning to have second thoughts about original) Mister Singer,
Copies to: Soviet Ministry of Trade, Import Section
           United States of America Ministry of Trade,
           Export Section
           United States of America Embassy, Moscow
           Soviet Foreign Ministry
           United States of America Foreign Ministry
           Chief Editor, The New York Times
           Chief Editor, Pravda
           Chief Editor, Newsweek magazine
           Chief Editor, Time magazine
           Chief Editor, L'Express
           E. Kennedy

I am honestly sorry to hear about your nail being pinched in the elevator door. Is it the kind of thing where you can sue the building, or are you the building? Soak the bruised nail in brine and wear a piece of malachite so it won't happen again, though the malachite must be given, never bought, for it to be at all effective. The rest of your nails sound conventional enough, though the way you clip them indicates you have an identity problem (maybe even a crisis) which is par for the course in an industrial society where we more often than not lose a sense of who we are and tend (if I have it right) to see ourselves as others see us, which is why we are all of us so different depending on whom we are with. As for your kind comments, they were generous and I appreciate them, really I do. I am embarrassed to admit I'm not at all sure if I'm an existentialist because I don't really remember what existentialism is. Funny as this sounds I learned it a dozen times if I learned it once, but each time I forget what I learned so that all I remember is that I understood it once but I can't for the life of me remember what I understood. I am an observer (there you are right on target) but only in the sense that your (I believe she was a fellow American) A. Toklas was an observer which is to say she liked a view but she liked to sit with her back turned to it. Here it is the only way to look at things and stay sane. Chez vous I suspect it is the same. But back to the business at hand, yes I would be willing to sign your waiver and I don't see who will be hurt if you tell the world you have a client in Moscow, though I would be careful if I were you and even if I weren't about using the phrase Iron Curtain because it would offend a great many people (myself included) who see more lack of difference than difference between what's on either side of this curtain. I'm not sure I understand why you are running into problems with the export license since it is hard for me to imagine that anybody in his or her right mind (assuming as I do that there are still people around who are in their right mind) would consider the Shuttle Race vital to the security of the United States of America. Perhaps I'm missing something here but do you manufacture anything other than sewing machines? Is the Shuttle Race interchangeable with some crucial piece of machinery on one of your phallic missiles or (what do they call them?) oh yes, jeeps? I must admit I have not actually taken time to look into the problem of acquiring an import license on this end, mainly because I have been terribly preoccupied with the activities of the attic with the pale nails I told you about who is trying (as a favor to me really) to show up as a plagiarist one of our well-known authors who shall for the moment remain name-less, though if the attic succeeds you will surely be reading about it in your darling New York Times. I promise though to take up the matter of the import license and to write to you as soon as I have any word. Until then I remain someone who greatly resents the fact that any vanguard feels it has the right to substitute its revolutionary consciousness for the con-sciousness (revolutionary or not) of the masses, of which I am a member.

Mother Russia

Post Scriptum: It strikes me rereading this that the difference between the written and the oral is that in the written you get no sense at all of my silences. Half a millimeter separates sentences but I crawl across the gap like a microscopic inch-worm, sometimes in an hour, sometimes (if I am preoc-cupied) in a day. Without a sense of my silences what can you know about me? Ha! Without my silences I am all talk. But that's another story.

2 May

Dear Mister Singer,
Copies to: Soviet Ministry of Trade, Import Section
           United States of America Ministry of Trade,
           Export Section
           United States of America Embassy, Moscow
           Soviet Foreign Ministry
           United States of America Foreign Ministry

Chief Editor, The New York Times
Chief Editor, Pravda
Chief Editor, Newsweek magazine
Chief Editor, Time magazine
Chief Editor, L'Express
E. Kennedy
J.-P. Sartre
A. Malraux
B. Russell
S. de Beauvoir
Amnesty International

For God's sake, forget the Shuttle Race. I don't want it any-more. You remember my attic with the pale nails I told you about, well he's been arrested. He was telling the truth in Red Square when they pounced on him. He is innocent and his arrest only proves what I always said, which is that innocence isn't pertinent anymore. I haven't the time to send you details of how he got where he got but only ask, even beg, you: HELP.

Mother Russia

Post Scriptum: I should have seen the handwriting on the wall when the blue-coated brutes let Vladimir Ilyich escape. But that's another story.

26 May

My very dear Mister Singer,
Copies to: Soviet Ministry of Trade, Import Section
United States of America Ministry of Trade, Export Section
United States of America Embassy, Moscow
Soviet Foreign Ministry
United States of America Foreign Ministry
Chief Editor, The New York Times

Chief Editor, Pravda
Chief Editor, Newsweek magazine
Chief Editor, Time magazine
Chief Editor, L'Express
E. Kennedy
J.-P. Sartre
A. Malraux
B. Russell
S. de Beauvoir
Amnesty International
Chief Psychiatrist, Soviet Ministry of Health
Chief Psychiatrist, United States of America
Ministry of Health
World Health Organization, Mental Department

Vladimir Ilyich (I apologize profusely for not explaining) is
Vladimir Ilyich Lenin, my parrot who flew the coop when the
boys in blue with their sad sagging eyelids and expressionless
mouths were searching for certain manuscripts which prove a
certain author is a plagiarist. As for my attic, he was, I found
out after several weeks of nosing (do you say the same thing?)
around, in an insane asylum, which is an institution the less
said about the better. A very greasy doctor with a mental
stutter who directed one of these state hotels once told me
in all seriousness that the great combats in the world are not
between Capitalists vs. Communists or haves vs. have-nots
or heads vs. hearts or blacks vs. whites or young vs. old or
warm vs. cold or south vs. north or even men vs. women but
(are you ready for this one?) oral vs. anal. This is not so of
course because as every sane person knows the great combats
in the world are between those who try and those who don't.
My attic tried and for his trouble was hauled off to the loony
bin on the grounds that an attempt to uncover a truth is

prima facie evidence of insanity, when everyone knows that insanity is really a question of where the majority is. Here I know from painful personal experience they can lock you in the bin and throw away the key for being too calm or too passionate or too sexy or too sexless. What (I put it to you) are irritability, neurasthenia, neurosis, hypochondria, anxiety, insomnia, agitation, absent-mindedness, eccentricity except manifestations of normality, but our hyenas of psychiatry (and I suspect yours too) take the absolutely scandalous view that people create the problems they enjoy not coping with and then lock them up for not coping. God help each and every one of us when we live in an epoch where eyebrows are raised if you are imaginative enough to see the world in a grain of sand and heaven in a wildflower. Well, I'm doing everything under the sun to get my attic out of the bin, which is why I don't understand at all your attitude about it being inappropriate for Singer to interfere in the internal affairs of another country. There is only one country in the world and we are all (God help us) in it. I've practically chained myself to my old Remington and fired off zingers to (among others) the head of the Soviet Academy of Science, the Chairman of the Council of Ministers, the Prosecutor General and my old slow-witted school chum who is, believe it or not, none other than the Secretary General of the Central Committee, little Leonid Brezhnev. So far all to no avail and I am getting desperate because (dear God, how can I explain it to you so you will understand?) my attic hasn't been charged with any crime, he has simply and utterly been swallowed by a building that seems to have more shadows than others. All this (I give you my word of honor as a Libra) because he knew something that was true and tried to tell others about it, because he tried to walk on water, move mountains, work up a sweat from a noneconomic activity, which now that I think about it is something you, dear Mister Singer, could do too. Hoping against hope that you can bring this matter to the attention of someone who can help I remain more than ever convinced that (in the words of our angelic Mendelstam) the earth for us has been worth a thousand heavens.

Mother Russia

Post Scriptum: Rereading your letters I can see you really don't understand my comment that the only way to observe life is to sit like A. Toklas with your back turned to it. Why I think this is because more often than not observing tends to distort what we are trying to observe and hence renders it unobservable. Like for instance a television camera at a mob scene, or better still a blind man trying to feel the shape and texture of a snowflake with his fingertips. From whence flows my theory that we are permitted (even obliged) to participate. But no just looking. But that's another story.

14 July

Mister Singer,
Copies to: Soviet Ministry of Trade, Import Section
United States of America Ministry of Trade,
Export Section
United States of America Embassy, Moscow
Soviet Foreign Ministry
United States of America Foreign Ministry
Chief Editor, The New York Times
Chief Editor, Pravda
Chief Editor, Newsweek magazine
Chief Editor, Time magazine
Chief Editor, L'Express
E. Kennedy

J.-P. Sartre
A. Malraux
B. Russell
S. de Beauvoir
Amnesty International
Chief Psychiatrist, Soviet Ministry of Health
Chief Psychiatrist, United States of America
Ministry of Health
World Health Organization, Mental Department
R. Nixon, President of the United States of America
L. Brezhnev, Secretary General of the
Central Committee of the Soviet Union

I ask you to excuse this long delay in answering your last
burst but I have my hands (and come to think of it my heart)
more or less full with my attic with the pale nails. He has
emerged, thanks God, from the building with more than its
share of shadows, in what condition I won't tell you, suffice it
to say that he wouldn't (or couldn't) talk except in his sleep.
He ran a fever which is gone now during which he tossed
and turned and ranted on about coming from the future or
the past (I'm not sure which) and shattered eyeglasses and
bucks never stopping and riding animals he was afraid to
identify. The single thing that I understood was that they had
tricked him (I'm still not sure how) into telling where he had
hidden the original manuscripts, which was in a snake pit
in a village near Moscow where an apprentice hustler raises
vipers to sell to the militia, which is something my attic did
when he was just starting out. As soon as he was up and around,
he took the electric train to the suburbs to make sure the
manuscripts were gone, which I don't need to tell you they
were, for which I was frankly just as happy because it meant
the affair was finished, only it wasn't. It wasn't because (and

*this I only just found out) the attic went to an American jour-
nalist he knows to get him to publish chez vous the truth
about the plagiarist, but the journalist said that rumors of the
plagiarism have been around for forty years and without proof
(which is to say without the original manuscripts) there was
nothing to be done. But he (if I have the sequence right) told
the attic he could put him in touch with someone who might
be able to help him get the manuscripts back and the attic,
with his skin now paler than his nails and all the time writing
notes instead of talking, said all right, though there was more
involved in organizing the meeting than simply agreeing to
it. The attic had to write a particular phrase on a particular
wall, something about how he's seen the future and it needs
work (whatever that means) after which he would find behind
a radiator in the lobby of a public building a slip of paper
giving him the time and place of the rendezvous, and it is
here that the story will interest you, Mister Singer, because
the rendezvous turned out (at least so the attic says) to be with
the new Moscow representative of the Singer Sewing Machine
Company, a man with a shiny bald scalp and long pinky nail
who said his name was Kolwradenor, which he jokingly explained stands for Kolchak-Wrangel-Denikin-Organizers of
Counter Revolution. Kolwradenor (are you still with me,
Mister Singer?) took the attic for a walk in a park where they
couldn't be overheard and told him that although there was no
possibility of regaining possession of the lost manuscripts he
(which is to say Kolwradenor) had friends who could fabricate
the manuscripts. To which my poor attic scribbled on a pad
that you couldn't prove a truth with a nontruth. To which
Kolwradenor replied that the lost manuscripts had been fabricated too. I will admit to you, I weep as I write this. The
lost manuscripts were fabricated! As for my attic, he removed his broken heart from the presence of the Singer Sewing Machine Company representative, who from my attic's*

description sounds like none other than Chuvash Al-hakim bi'amrillahi, the seventy-first incarnation of God, and also Melor, a certain KGB interrogator, all wrapped up into one. For a long while I thought my attic was off his rocker and inventing all of the above. You, my dear sheltered Mister Singer, will probably think we're both stark raving, my attic and me, but we finally figured it all out and here it is: Your CIA and our KGB are the same organization, there is no other explanation for it. And Kolwradenor-Melor-Chuvash is their Moscow bureau chief. Which has the advantage of cutting down on overhead and salaries and permitting a degree of coordination that wouldn't be possible if they had separate offices. Being a businessman yourself you will appreciate the cost-effectiveness of the scheme immediately. It was Kolwradenor (I'll bet my remaining parrots) who organized it so we would all wind up in the same house and then dropped the fabricated manuscripts in our collective laps. Why? I can hear you asking. My guess is that it wasn't to expose the plagiarism (what does he care about plagiarism?) but to set the bosses on the Politburo against each other. I'm as certain of it as I am that I am perfectly sane that your CIA meant for it to be discovered that the manuscripts were fabricated, and that it was the falsity which would cause the dissension, since one side would assume the other had fabricated the evidence in order to discredit it. Melor of course was simply playing the game and doing his best to avoid the dissension by preventing the manuscripts (which he knew were fabricated) from surfacing. My attic asked Kolwradenor what his bosses would do to him now that he had failed and he claims Kolwradenor replied that since the combat in the world is the Intelligence people vs. Everyone, he had nothing to worry about inasmuch as it is the intelligence people who decide between themselves who will win what round, the important thing being to keep the game going. All of which (you can imagine, can't you?) left my attic in quite a fragile state, so much so that he wrote across Kolwradenor's door with some kind of cream he squeezed from a tube that he hoped in his next incarnation he would again be a victim. On his way back here the attic spotted by chance in a pharmacy window a new product called the cotton toothpick, which turns out to be the very same Q-Tips I told you about (do you remember?) some letters back. It seems they are quite poor specimens inasmuch as there is not enough cotton at the points, which are in any case dangerously sharp. A thousand applications is what the publicity boasted, but there was one they never imagined in their wildest moments. The attic (poor dear) was very agitated, he kept asking how can you prove a truth with a nontruth? and writing that there were some things in the world which he couldn't bear to hear. Right there in front of my eyes (do you have a strong stomach, Mister Singer?) he punctured his ear drums with the sharp tips of the cotton toothpicks. First one, then the other. He didn't bleed very much you'll be relieved to know, but it was extremely painful and he did make himself deaf, which has a certain symmetry because the only one in the world he really wants to hear isn't able to speak. The newfound deafness drove him into a depression from which he seems (thanks God) to be finally emerging, though he still doesn't touch wood. He has started learning to lip-read and only yesterday, smiling in a way I had never seen him smile before, he handed me a note saying something about how if Q-Tips come can vaginal deodorant spray be far behind. Trusting you too, dear Mister Singer, will be a victim in your next incarnation I remain

Mother Russia

Post Scriptum: It dawns on me I never told you very much (come to think of it anything) about the house in which I live.

It is the (excuse the expression) cul of an L-shaped cul-de-sac. The structure as far as I can judge through my bifocals has no straight lines, no sharp edges, only worn angles and soft sexy shadows. The windows, some of which have eucalyptus branches on the sills stare out at the alleyway like bruised eyes, which is not unreasonable considering the house has seen more than most. In winter it leans into the winds that cut through the cul-de-sac. In summer it leans into winds that aren't blowing. Inside it smells of sandalwood and peeling wallpaper and fireplaces that don't draw. I mustn't forget to mention the floors creak under foot. The stairs too. I am moved to tell you all this because in one of the silences between sentences (ha! you see I am not all talk!) the sound of hammering reached my ears. Naturally I went down to see what was going on. Everyone who lives in the house was milling excitedly around a piece of paper that had just been tacked to a tree. My attic angrily scrawled across it, Quis custodiet ipsos custodes? What language is that, Jewish? asked a pretty young thing called Ophelia Long Legs. The paper served notice that the bosses who deal with such things have decided to tear down the last wooden house in central Moscow. To construct an enormous high-rise asylum. But that's another story.

Or is it?